Pieces of the Hole

Pieces of the Hole

by Tony Lindsay

THIRD WORLD PRESS

Chicago

Third World Press
Publishers since 1967
Chicago

First Edition
Printed in the United States of America

Cover design by Keir Thirus
Layout and interior design by Mode Infotech LLC

Library of Congress Control Number: 2008901506
ISBN-10 0-88378-269-3
ISBN-13 978-0-88378-269-9

12 11 10 09 08 07   6 5 4 3 2 1

Table of Contents

I. Part One: Old Folks and City Kids

1. Macky's Place   3

2. The Panties Lesson   21

3. Real Life   25

4. The Mailman's Cherry Grove Blues   53

5. Things Done Changed   63

6. A Broken Rule   67

7. Life on T.V.   77

8. Our Dance   87

9. Paid Fo'   95

10. Old Folks' Home   105

11. Mama and Santa Claus   111

II. Part Two: A Lil' Twisted

1. Brotherly Love   119

2. The Finishing Place   125

3. A Brother's Death   132

4. My Father's Day   134

5. Time to Go   140

6. A Memorable Elevator Ride   155

7. A Day in the Park   158

8. Home Grown   167

9. Marc on Mark   173

PART ONE

Old Folks and City Kids

I

Macky's Place

Macky's Place is not distinct from hundreds of other South Side bars in Chicago. It has a single mahogany bar facing a wall width mirror. Below the lighted mirror is a long shelf that holds an array of colored glass bottles filled with liquid spirits.

The leather top bar stools at Macky's have seen better days because Macky brought them second hand and worn. The brass foot railing of the bar hasn't been polished since the bar was named "The Irish Rose" and the same carpet that covered the floor boards of the Irish Rose in '67 hides the floor at Macky's in 2005. Macky is not known for his renovations; what he is known for are his constant conversations, unwavering opinions, and good corn liquor.

Macon Taylor bought the bar after he retired from the Chicago Board of Education in '89; he was sixty-five-years old. He would have retired at sixty-two, but he didn't want to be home alone. He waited for his wife to retire, so he would have someone to talk with throughout the day.

While he was the janitor at Nicholas Copernicus Elementary School, he spent a good part of his day talking. His favorite conversations were with the students and what he enjoyed most was surprising them with historical facts about Chicago. None knew about the blizzard in '67, the riots '19, or about the Indian tribes that once inhabited the area. Most of the students didn't care much about past events, but they all showed an interest in hearing about the Indians. Passing a little history along either to children or uninformed patrons at his bar is one of Macky's life passions; another is the distilling of quality corn liquor.

His granddaddy and daddy were both bootleggers and producing the family recipe was a trade that had been passed down for three generations. Macky's son dying in Vietnam stopped the tradition.

It was said that Macky's corn liquor was the best in the city. He knew it was the illegal shots of the liquor not his knowledgeable conversation that kept a lot of the regulars coming to the bar. Macky only sells shots while the bar is open, but after hours he sells pints and gallons from his second floor apartment across the street.

He moved into the apartment after Celestine, his wife of thirty-five years, died. Despite his daughter's protest, he sold their suburban home shortly after his wife's death and returned to the city. His daughter, Elizabeth, felt the suburbs were better for her aging father and tried her best to stop him from moving back to 71st Street.

Macky left the city decades ago only because Celestine wanted to raise their two children in the suburbs. With Celestine and his son, Thomas, gone and Elizabeth married and mother to her own children, Macky figured he could live where he wanted, so his daughter's protest fell on deaf ears.

He was born in Chicago and spent his childhood in a gray stone building on 54th and Indiana. When his father started working at Sabastine's hardware store, the family moved to 71st Street. Eventually, his uncle and father brought the hardware store and the family moved above it. The hardware store is now a barbecue joint and Macky still owns the building. He rents out the larger front apartment that his family once lived in.

His renter, Veronica, is a nice young woman with five children; he rented her the apartment after she came to his bar with plate of spaghetti and chitterlings. At the time, he was living in the larger three-bedroom apartment in the front of the building. She came into the bar dressed in blue jeans, white gym shoes and a white sweatshirt. She sat on a stool and put the plate of hot food in front him. He'd just opened the bar that day, so he and his pit bull, Caesar, were the only people there.

The aroma that rose from the plate told him she knew how to use spices, garlic and onions. He wasn't the type of man who ate everyone's cooking, especially other people's chitterlings, but the aroma got the best of his caution. Veronica uncovered the plate without a word and handed him a fork.

He'd seen her and her five children on 71st Street before. Quite a sight they made walking down the street, all six of them a little over-weight and short—a chubby mother with five chubby children.

While he was eating, she told him how she'd been sick with asthma and was two days away from being evicted because she hadn't paid her rent. Her nonpayment of rent was not totally due to her sickness. She liked to gamble some and had had a bad streak of luck. She assured him that she was working on the gambling with all her heart and soul. She swore that if she was given a break, she would never put her children at risk of being set out again. She told him how she got into the bad situation she was in was due to her own stupidity. She received a monthly check that was big enough to take care of all her five children. What she needed was an apartment to move into that wouldn't require a security deposit.

She had heard from Nathan, the handyman that Macky employed, about a small place above the rib joint. She knew it was too small for her and her five children, but she only needed a place to stay until she got her money together; a place that would stop her from going to a homeless shelter.

Macky, who had been eating and listening, looked into the round face of Veronica. He saw eyes that he thought were honest and sincere. While he was forking up the last of the chitterlings and spaghetti, she added that she cooked every day and that he could expect a plate daily and a real good meal on Sundays. That clinched the deal for him because the plate of food she offered reminded him of Celestine's cooking.

Macky moved into the smaller unit in the back and gave Veronica and her children the larger front unit. The move turned out to be better for him because of his "three a.m." corn liquor customers. The customers could park in the alley and walk straight up the back stairs. Once upstairs, they would make their purchase and leave barely noticed. The move benefited him and Veronica both.

If Veronica still had a gambling problem, it didn't show in her affairs. During the two years she rented from him, she never missed a rent payment or a plate and she kept her kids quiet and clean. That's why when she came into the bar on a Friday night, his busy night, to talk to him about his grandson, he gave her his ear.

Every stool at the bar is occupied and people are standing behind people trying to get drinks. Macky is at the end of the bar dressed in his customary white button down shirt, black dress slacks, gray suspenders and black Stacy Adams lace ups. His arthritis stops him from ironing and pressing the cotton shirts like he did for most of his years. Now he sends them to the laundry to get cleaned, pressed and starched.

The ailment also stops him from pouring drinks on his busiest night; he simply can't keep up with the fast pace the Friday night crowd demands, so he hired two pretty bartenders for the weekend shifts. Renee' and Regina are sisters that are three years apart, but most people mistake them for twins. The pretty sisters had owned their own bar in the neighborhood, but mismanagement and back taxes put them out of business a year ago. The sisters' popularity in the neighborhood added to Macky's already busy Friday night. For fifty plus year-old women the sisters are very shapely and dress to draw attention to their curvy hips and healthy bosoms. More than a couple of the weekend patrons are their suitors.

Looking over the crowd, Macky guesses about fifty percent of the customers are due to the sisters. He smiles as he watches them skillfully pouring shots. When he told them about the corn liquor shots, all they wanted to know was what their end would be.

Whatever the news, Veronica is upset. Standing silently Macky watches as she fidgets with the jewelry on her wrist and fingers instead of talking to him. He gave her a free beer, which she hasn't touched. Macky is standing at the end of the bar leaning heavily on it because he gave her his stool as well. The small of his back is tightening from leaning on the bar. His tall frame isn't suited for the bent position he is in.

Through the buzz of the Friday night patrons he hears Veronica whisper, "I think . . . no, Mr. Taylor, I know your grandson is selling rocks behind our building. He does it out of his car."

Macky leans towards her, "Rocks?"

She looks up from her jewelry and into the dark green lenses of Macky's eyeglasses, "Drugs, Mr. Taylor, cocaine."

"Tyrese?" He stood straight up from the bar. Last he heard, the boy was doing all the right things. What Veronica is telling him doesn't make sense.

"Yes sir, it's him and two other boys. They sell up until it's about time for you to close the bar, before your after hours customers start coming to the alley.

"Mr. Taylor, my kids play in that small back yard and if it wasn't for that, I wouldn't say a word to you, but I don't want them to get hurt. Selling rocks always brings some kind of trouble like shootings, beatings; something bad always happens. I tried to talk to Tyrese, but he told me to mind my own business. Mr. Taylor, having a safe place for my children to play is my business."

She stands from the bar stool and drinks down the beer, "If you walk over there now, Mr. Taylor, you can see for yourself. Goodnight now . . . and I ain't telling you this to start no trouble. I'm trying to stop trouble."

Standing taller than most of the crowd, Macky is able to watch her wobble through the customers and out the door.

Tyrese is a seventeen-year old high school senior who has already been accepted to the University of Chicago. He was raised in the south suburbs and still lives out there with his mother and father. Lately, Macky has been seeing the kid a lot on 71st Street but he figured the boy had found himself a girlfriend in the neighborhood.

The truth be told Macky, was happy to see more of the lanky boy, who walked just like his son did at that age; Tyrese walked with long steps that would take an average man two to keep up. Both his son and his grandson got his family's height. They were tall men. Tyrese even smiled like him and Thomas. Seeing the boy brought joy to Macky's heart.

Why would the boy be selling drugs?

Macky returns to sitting on his stool. He knew the answer to the question: fast money. The same reason he'd sold corn liquor when he

had a good job with the Board of Education. Having extra money
never hurt him, it wasn't hurting him now. Matter of fact the corn
liquor money was what he was planning on using to help Elizabeth
with Tyrese's tuition.

Sitting five stools down from him at the bar was Nathan, his
handyman and brew assistant. He knew Nathan was spending time up
at Veronica's - a great deal of time. He figured if something was bothering Veronica, Nathan knew about. He looked at Nathan long
enough to catch his eye; with a nod of the head Macky signaled for
him to meet him in the back office. Nathan gave an agreeing nod and
drained his beer. Macky rose slowly from the stool and walked toward
the back office. Nathan was beside him.

"Arthur with you today, Mr. Taylor?"

"Yes, buddy, he rode down on me this morning something fierce
and been riding me ever since. You would think as busy as I stayed
most of my life, the good Lord wouldn't have gave me an ailment
that slows me down. He knows I got to move around, but maybe
me moving around so much is what he's trying to stop. Who
knows?

"But I sent off for some herbs I read about last week from Asia and
from what I read on the Internet, they just might be some help. I read
about something to help you with that gout too. I ordered it for you."

"Why, thank you, Mr. Taylor. If they work half as good as them
roots you gave me to help me sleep, I'll be on to something."

When they reach the windowless back office, which doubles as a
storeroom, Macky sits on high-stacked cases of canned beer and
Nathan, who remains standing, pulls the door close. It's a small room
made tight with bar stock. Macky's eyes immediately go to a mouse
scurrying into a hole in a corner. Macky has been seeing the mice for
about six months and doesn't have a big problem because he enjoys
watching Caesar chase them through the place.

"You saw me talking with Veronica?" Macky looks through the
dark green lenses of his bifocals to Nathan.

"Yes, sir."

"And?"

"She's telling you the truth, Mr. Taylor, him and his boys been back there a couple weeks. They get back there about three thirty, four in the afternoon and go up until the time for you to close the bar."

"Is Tyrese in charge?"

"That's how it looks, sir. I see them turning over the money to him. He'll leave one or two of them sitting in his car while he goes off. He works the last couple of hours himself." He looks down at his watch, "He probably out there now, sir."

The thought of walking across the street, then down the block and around to the alley wasn't an appealing thought, but Nathan obviously wanted him to see Tyrese with his own eyes.

"Is your car out front?"

"Yes, sir."

"Will you drive me around there?"

"No problem, Mr. Taylor."

"All right then, meet me out front in a minute."

With Nathan gone, Macky sits quiet for a minute. Life has always had work for him. This is a problem he is sure that his conservative daughter and son-in-law could not handle. They would either have Tyrese arrested or sent him to a psychiatrist. It was obvious to Macky that the problem was purely financial.

Before Macky got up from the stacked cases, he began formulating a plan in his mind, one that could serve his need and Tyrese's, especially, since the boy was already showing bootlegger tendencies, might as well point him in the right direction.

Before leaving the bar, Macky went behind the mahogany counter and got his .38 pistol, just in case. He also thought about taking Caesar out from behind the bar to get some night air, but thought better of it since he and Nathan both would be gone, he left Caesar for security.

When they turned into the alley, Macky had Nathan park against a garage a few houses down from his grandson's parked car. The boy has quite a business going, a steady stream of people are walking up the alley to his car.

"How long you say he's been in business?"

"Three weeks at the most."

"Looks like he's doing pretty good for himself."

"This ain't nothing Mr. Taylor, sometimes they have folks lined up."

"Lined up? Don't that attract the police?"

"Not yet, but it will."

"And how much does what he sell cost?"

"Ten dollars a rock."

"Do you use that stuff?"

"No! I can't afford a habit like that. Folks spend they whole checks on that mess."

Macky sat and watched over forty people walk to his grandson's car. His corn liquor business with the shots sold in bar made about eight hundred a week. He figured his grandson business was doing better than that in a day. The boy could pay for his own college tuition if he didn't go to jail first.

"Cut your lights on pull up alongside the car."

After Nathan pulled parallel with Tyrese's parked car, Macky climbs out with his .38 on his side. He anchors himself on Nathan's '76 Ford LTD and slowly walks around to the Toyota Celica he bought his grandson.

He taps on the driver's window with the .38. People continue to walk up to the car even with him standing there. When his grandson rolls the window down, Macky feels a blast of cold air from the air conditioner. It isn't hot enough to be running the air. It's a nice cool August night; the kid is wasting money Macky thinks. Once the window is rolled all the way down, Macky sees a shocked crooked smile that could have been on his son face.

"Hey, Papa." Tyrese says.

"Boy, get out of this alley and meet me back at the bar. And damn it, I mean right now! No, better yet, open up the door and drive me around to the bar."

Macky turns to Nathan's car and yells, "Go on back around front. I'm a ride back with my grandson."

Macky makes it around to the passenger door of the Toyota. When he gets to the door, he sees an embarrassed young lady trying to pull her clothes together. She slides past him without saying a word.

The car is low to the ground. Macky knows he will need help getting out of it. When he finally gets in he says, "Get on around to the bar before I smack your ass upside the head with my pistol." And after stooping to get in the car, he is mad enough to do it.

Between his grandson's legs he sees two paper sacks; one is filled with little tiny plastics bags with white chips inside of them. Macky guesses that these are rocks. The other bag is filled to the brim with cash. He reaches over and grabs them both and with a disciplining gaze, he dares his grandson to say a word.

Tyrese has to park in the bus stop at the corner because Macky's customers have occupied all the parks in front of the bar.

"Get on around to this door; you're going to have to help me out of this here car," he orders.

His grandson is a thin boy but Macky feels his strength as he anchors against him to rise out of the Celica. Standing he and his grandson are the same height, he looks into the boys brown eye's and says, "So you a drug dealer now huh?"

"No Papa, not really."

"Ain't this drugs in this here bag? Never mind, come on inside with me."

Nathan walks up on them and Macky tells his grandson, "Give him the keys to the car, it will be awhile before you be driving that little machine. The title is still in my name."

His grandson's mouth drops open. Macky ignores his unspoken protest and continues, "Nathan, take it around to the garage and park it next to the kettle, I think there is enough room."

Hesitating to hand the keys over, Tyrese says, "Papa, I'm a need my car to drive home."

"You ain't going home tonight, so that ain't your worry; give him the keys."

Reluctantly, he hands him them over.

Walking to the bar Macky notices Tyrese has slowed the pace of his walk for him and the boy had nerve to be smiling a little bit but Macky couldn't get mad at the smile because he is smiling too. The two like being in each other's company, they always have and it has always shown.

"How you feelin,' Papa?"

"Could be better, a little stiff."

"Papa, I not a drug dealer."

Macky feels Tyrese trying to look into his eye, but he continues to look straight ahead.

"If you give me a minute to explain, you'll understand."

"Later."

When they get into the bar, he tells Tyrese, "Get on behind bar and start on that sink of dishes and don't leave from it."

Macky makes it to his stool at the end of the bar and sits. To the bartending sisters he says, "Y'all got a dish washer tonight, so keep the drinks flowing. Don't neither one of y'all touch a glass. He's washing for the night."

Keeping the paper bags in front of him, he folds them over to prevent anyone from looking inside. He shakes his head at his grandson who is dressed in a pair blue jeans four sizes too big and a white t-shirt equally oversized. He looks more like a thug than a college-bound senior. Macky flips open his cell phone and dials his daughter's home number.

"Hey, Beth . . . Oh, everything's fine. I'm calling to tell you Tyrese is spending the night with me . . . his board up service job . . . Oh, they got sent home early, so he stopped by the bar to see me . . . Well, since I own the joint, I think I'll risk breaking the no minors law . . . Just letting you know he's with me . . . Love you too, baby."

Macky signals for a double shot of corn liquor and pulls from his shirt pocket one of his last Cuban cigars. It was Tyrese who directed him to the website that shipped him the only box of Cuban cigars he ever had. The site disappeared from the web soon after Macky got his order, so he cherishes the cigars and lights them sparingly.

This problem with Tyrese is bigger than he thought; the kid is making real money. When his father started him on the kettle, he was washing out stalls at the stable, so the corn liquor money was big time for him and he knew from birth that one day the family business would be his.

Tyrese knew very little of his business and had no expectations of taking it over. The truth be told Macky was thinking about giving the recipe to Nathan, who'd been his assistant for over ten years and knew everything but the proportions of the ingredients.

Macky is rolling the tip of the Cuban cigar around in his mouth thinking – the boy is probably splitting the drug money three ways. The corn liquor money would be all his and the hours were a lot less, brew for two days distribute for ten and it only takes a couple hours a day to distribute.

Macky would still pour the shots in the bar for him, so he wouldn't have to work in the bar, just serve the after hour customers a couple of hours a night. Easy money any way a person looked at it.

Nathan is walking into the front of the bar, "Nathan, come here." Macky yells through the rumble of the bar. He watches his assistant make it through the shoulder-to-shoulder crowd to him. Over the years, Nathan had become more friend than assistant.

"It was more than enough room, we could get another one of them little ole cars in there."

"That's good . . . Listen here, Nathan. What are your plans with the corn liquor business?"

"I ain't got no plans sir, I just do as I'm told."

"I know that, but do you want something out of it for yourself? Would you like to one day run the whole thing?"

Without hesitation Nathan answers "No, Mr. Taylor, I wouldn't. I don't want the responsibility you have. If something goes wrong with a batch, people coming after you, not me and I like it like that."

"You happy with your share?"

"The money's fine, it always has been. I ain't got no problems with nothing. You got a problem with me?"

"No, no, not at all. I'm just thinking about turning it all over to Tyrese, to get him out that alley."

"Do he know how to cook?"

"No, that we will have to teach him, along with everything else."

Nathan looks towards Tyrese, who is bent over with his hands in the sink filled with sudsy water, "If he got half a brain, he'd rather sell corn liquor than those rocks. Don't hardly nobody go to jail for selling corn liquor no more, but damn near all them baggy pants boys go to jail for selling them rocks."

"That's true, but the boy is making money. I got a sack of it right here." He picks up one of the brown paper bag and drops it the bar top.

"Big money, big risk, Mr. Taylor. Tyrese ain't a dumb boy."

"That's what I'm hoping, Nathan. I truly am."

A stool opens up next to Macky and Nathan sits.

"How much he know about the business now?"

"Just the stories about the old days down South with my daddy and granddaddy."

"Well, he must know something about now because he got sense enough to stop doing his business before your business starts."

Rolling the Cuban cigar around on his lips, Macky says, "You got a point there, Nathan."

One of the sisters comes over to them with a double shot for Macky. "Now you know better than putting that fine, young, slim, 'thang' back here with us. I'll have him growing up faster than you want, Macky." She says with sly smile and wink of the eye. "Looking at him makes me think about how fine you must have been as a young man."

"What you talking about 'must have been?' Little sister, I'm good looking man now. Don't you know that in most tribal communities, men ain't considered worthy until after sixty?"

She leans over the counter top to Macky and places her hand on top of his, "Don't get me wrong, Macky. I know you are good looking worthy man, but a worthy man is not always what a woman wants. It's a man who has it working . . . Now, that's what I want, and that grandbaby of yours . . . mmph, mmph, he got it working in a big way."

Looking into the cleavage that the sister's deeply vee'd blouse displayed, Macky tightens their handclasp and answers, "Worthy, my darling, not only means working, but it means working with experience."

He lifts her hand to his lips and kisses it.

"You need to come on over to my place one of these mornings and experience a worthy man, you might just like it."

It is now Macky's turn to offer a sly grin.

"You better stop!" She yanks her hand away and steps back. "I ain't about to mix business with pleasure with you. I heard about you having bar maids in here working for free. You ain't about to work whatever you worked on them on me, no sir, Mr. Man!" She turns her back on them and walks to the other end with her sister.

Watching the roll of her butt Nathan says, "Them is two stacked sisters."

"That they are, buddy, that they truly are," Macky agrees while rolling the unlit Cuban cigar over his lips, "So, you ain't got a problem with me bringing Tyrese on?"

"None at all, it's better than what he's doing now and I could use the help."

"You sure now?"

"Yeah, I'm sho'."

Nathan answers which such certainty that Macky turns to look at him and what he sees surprises him. He sees a man that looks at least ten years older than the man he hired. When he hired Nathan, he had to be close to fifty. Like him, Nathan has aged.

When Nathan was hired, Macky helped with most of the lifting and hauling. Macky couldn't remember the last time he lifted a sack of corn. Nathan did all the labor and, of course, he needed help. Why hadn't he seen how old Nathan had become?

The bar closed a half hour later than usual. Folks just didn't want to leave. The sisters had to physically push the last four customers out the door. And with very little coaxing Nathan agreed to drive the sister home. The only ones left are Caesar, Tyrese, and Macky in the bar and Cesar is busy chasing mice. Tyrese draws himself a pitcher of SevenUP, comes from around the bar and sits on the stool to left of Macky.

"Papa, I'm tired. My back hurts, my feet ache and my shoulders are sore. I don't see how the sisters do it. I wasn't back there half the time they were."

"They're used to it . . . they probably would get tired real fast if they had to sit up in a little car in the alley and sell drugs for hours."

Macky still hadn't lit the cigar. Tyrese pulls a book of matches from the ashtray in front of Macky, he lights two of them and offers the flame to his grandfather. Macky sticks the tip of the cigar into the flame and puffs.

"Oh . . . so, we getting ready to talk about that?" Tyrese blows out the matches.

"Yes, I think it's time we talk about that." Macky releases a huge cloud of smoke and opens the brown bag that is stuffed with the rocks. "This is a bag full of drugs and you were selling them behind my building. I know this because I sat and watched people come up to the car I bought . . . and purchase this mess from you. To me that looks like you are a drug dealer."

The cigar tip is glowing.

"I sold drugs, that's true, but I'm not a drug dealer. You see I was only doing it to make some money for school; drugs dealers sell drugs for life. I was trying to get me enough money to do things a little better than how mom and dad are doing them."

"What do you mean?"

"OK, it's like this; they bought me a PC right, instead of a laptop. Every kid on every college campus has a laptop unless they are poor and from the inner city. Even with the phone - they bought me a regular cell phone instead of a picture phone. How am I suppose to receive pictures? And it doesn't stop there Papa, a tiny tube television instead of a small plasma screen, and I can't even began to tell you how foul the clothes are they bought me.

"Daddy told me yesterday the most I could expect was two hundred dollars a month cash from them while I'm on campus. Papa, that will be gone in a week. I know they are doing the best they can, that's why I decided to do what I can because I can do better. I made enough to buy all the right stuff and put eight thousand in the bank.

"It's going to be kids coming from all over the country on that campus. I'm not going to be the poor kid from the inner city, Papa.

I got the grades to make me equal, now I got the things. Hey! You are giving me my Celica back, right?"

Macky saw him trying to look past his dark lenses into his eyes. All Tyrese could see was the glow of the cigar reflecting in the bottom half of the lenses.

"Who are you trying to be equal to son?" His grandson sounded spoiled rotten to him and he had done a great deal of the spoiling. Whenever he gave the boy something, he always told him a man got his own and the sooner he started getting his own, the sooner he would be a man.

"Mostly the rich kids, Papa. All through high school they had better stuff. I wasn't having it in college." Tyrese poured himself a tall glass of the SevenUP and gulped.

"You are willing to risk jail to have these things?" He mashed the cigar out in the ashtray, less than an inch of it had been smoked.

Wiping his mouth Tyrese answered, "It really wasn't a big risk Papa, everybody knows you pay the cops to stay away from that alley."

"Every cop ain't crooked, son, and my customers know that they still have to be careful. That alley is not a safe haven and it's only partially safe after three am. What I do for Sergeant doesn't protect that alley twenty-four hours a day. Who told you such foolishness?"

"Papa, I been hearing it all my life, people say you own this whole block. They say the police captain and the alderman are in your hip pocket and that you supply the whole South Side with corn liquor."

Macky removes his glasses and looks his grandson straight in the eyes.

"Boy, don't you know to ask me about what people say concerning me? I own two buildings on this block - two. And I couldn't tell you the police captain's name if you put a pistol to my head. I don't know the man.

"Yes, I throw the alderman a barbecue every year because it's smart to have a politician think of you as a friend, but he ain't in my pocket. Old Sergeant and a couple of his buddies drink here free, so they keep an eye on the alley for me. But I ain't bought a safe haven."

Macky slips his glasses back on, pulls his gold Zippo lighter from his pants pocket, and relights the cigar.

"Now, I do have the best corn liquor on the South Side and I do supply most of it, not all of it, but most of it. I'm not a gangster, son. I don't pay the police off and I don't hob knob with politicians. I'm a bar owner who also bootlegs. That's it and that's all."

Macky blows three smoke rings from his mouth.

"If the police would have caught you back there in that alley selling drugs, it wouldn't have been a damn thing I could have done except get you a lawyer."

"For real, Papa? That alley is not protected?"

"No."

His grandson looks honestly shocked and a bit scared. "Justifiably so," Macky thinks.

"You mean, I could have went to jail?"

"And fucked up your life." He blows a big puff of smoke in his grandsons face and flipps his lighter closed.

Coughing Tyrese says, "Aw, man. I thought it was protected, Papa I really did. I not only put myself at risk, but I put my boys at risk too. Tony has a juvenile drug conviction that hasn't cleared. He really didn't want to do it, but I talked him into it by telling him how safe it was."

"The Lord watches out for fools and babies and you are still a little bit of both." Macky releases a smoke ring that grows to the size of a Christmas wreath; they both watch it.

"So, I guess it's safe to say I won't be seeing you out there again?"

"No, not again. This was our last night anyway, each of us made what we needed. In two weeks we will all be away at school. Well, I won't be far away, but still away."

"So your illegal activities are over?" Macky avoids looking up as he puts out the Cuban cigar.

"Papa, I'm not even going to jaywalk."

He wants to ask his grandson if he is sure, but instead he says, "You know you can come to me for things you want and need."

"Papa, you bought me the car and you are always saying the sooner a boy stands on his own, the sooner he is a man."

Macky leans closer to his grandson and rest his arm across the back of his shoulders. "Come to me next time. I always have something around here for you to do, and I pay pretty good. Here, take your money, but I'm keeping the drugs since you said you and your guys were finished. Right?"

"Keep them, Papa I don't care. We don't owe nobody for them; we were selling two for one tonight anyway . . . but what about my car Papa?"

Macky has him almost cheek-to-cheek in the embrace, "Oh, you'll get that back after you apologize to Veronica, and the way you are going to apologize is that you are going to take her and her five kids shopping tomorrow. I'm going to let you use my Lincoln and you are going to spend at least a thousand dollars of your money on them.

"A thousand, Papa!" Tyrese tries to move out of the cheek to cheek embrace, but Macky holds him close.

"You totally disrespected that woman and you will not get your car back until she accepts your apology. Understand me, boy?"

"Yes, Papa."

Macky releases him.

"OK, now be the good grandson that you are and take Caesar for a walk before you go upstairs. I'm going to wait here for Nathan." Just as Macky spoke Nathan walks in, "speak of the Devil and he will appear."

"Caesar, come here boy. You ready for a walk?" Tyrese calls out. The gray and black pit bull bolts from the backroom to Tyrese, who grabs the leash from under the counter. "Papa, I don't have keys to your place."

"I don't lock my doors son, people know better." They smiled at each other as Tyrese walks out the bar. Nathan goes behind the bar and draws himself a beer.

"So is he in?"

"No. He's got my blood, but he's also has his mama and his daddy and the suburbs in him. He's a good kid going to college. Here." He throws him the bag of rocks. "I think we need to find out a little bit more about these, they weigh a hell of a lot less than a sack of corn."

"Mr. Taylor, no!"

"I was just messing with you unless you want to do it? No, I'm just playing . . . but you are going to have to find yourself a brew assistant because you're being promoted to cook."

"Cook, that means you will have to give me the recipe."

"Yep, that's what that means. Don't worry. I'll be right there with you for awhile. We won't tell nobody that it's you cooking until you comfortable with it and after awhile it will be all yours."

"Mr. Taylor, I don't want all that on me."

"Try it on first Nathan, see if it fits. If it don't, you can always walk away. Throw me them rocks back. Maybe old Sergeant can do something with them."

2

The Panties Lesson

I was eight years old when I learned my panties lesson and like many predicaments of my childhood I was following Franklin Benton—the older kid next door who my parents thought was responsible enough to walk me to school. They were wrong.

Franklin was a curious kid with a criminal nature and when he clicked into either his investigate or get paid mode, he didn't consider what was best for himself or me. On more than one occasion our two-block walk to school ended with us either in the principal's office or in the back of a police squad car.

Even though he was three years older than me, Franklin kept a snotty nose and wore thick glasses and was the target of a lot pubescent teasing. He wasn't my best buddy, but I think I was his. His interests at the time of my panties lesson revolved around girls.

On that bright spring day he approached me during recess. He pulled me away from my class buddies and whispered to me his idea of sneaking into the gym during the sixth grade girls' sex education class. Initially, I had no interest. It was spring, we were outside at recess, and it was going to be my turn to choose teams for kickball. Sneaking back into the school didn't sound like a good idea at all.

I was anxious to get away from Franklin and back to my own classmates until he explained what sneaking in the gym would allow us to see. He baited me with an opportunity few third grade boys would turn down, a chance to see some panties.

He told me that if we hid under the bleachers in the gym, we would get to see all the sixth grade girls' panties because they would be seating above us. It sounded like a good plan to me, except for sneaking away from the playground meant missing recess and kickball.

Kickball was the one game I was really good at. A kid didn't have to be tall, burly, or a good runner to play. All a kid had to do was be able to kick a ball and run a little. It was my favorite game; but, the thought of being able to tell my buddies that I saw all the sixth grade girls' panties did seem like a better deal. I was in.

We were successful in leaving the sunny playground undetected and slithering between the gym doors into the dark gymnasium was a breeze. Getting under the bleachers was easy enough too. The problem I noticed was that the gym was dark and beneath the bleachers all we could see was the back of the girls legs and their shoes. The gym was full of girls, however, and they were watching a movie about girl stuff.

I turned to leave because of the darkness, but Franklin grabbed a hold of my arm and told me to wait. He whispered assurance that when the lights came on the girls would stand and we would see all their panties. Held by the possibility of seeing the treasure no boy in my class had seen before, I stayed and began watching the film.

What I understood from the film was that girls grew eggs inside them and the eggs were full of blood. When the eggs fell out of the girls, they cracked open and the girls had to catch them in this big band aid, and then, put the whole mess in a little blue bag.

It all seemed really gross to me. I remembered my mother telling me that eggs with a lot of blood in them were no good for cooking, so the eggs these girls were growing had to be ruined. I was glad my mother brought our eggs from the supermarket.

Crouched under the bleachers panic suddenly took me. It occurred to me that we were beneath a whole lot of girls and at any moment their eggs might slip out and land on us. That thought motivated me towards the gym doors, but just as I crawled from underneath the bleachers the lights came on and fat Anita Stein and her fatter twin sister Claries screamed, "A boy; there's a boy in here!"

In a matter of seconds girls surrounded me. They were hitting me, and kicking me, and calling me nasty. I couldn't believe they were calling me nasty. I wasn't the one growing ruined eggs inside of me.

I really wanted to hit fat Anita in her stomach and make her eggs crack open since she was the one hitting me the hardest and the most, but my father told me never to hit a girl. So, I didn't throw one of the punches he taught me, instead I covered up and blocked as many balled up fists as I could.

When the teacher finally got to me, I was beat up pretty bad and confused as to why the girls attacked me. I saw Franklin running out the gym doors unnoticed and untouched. Old mean Mrs. Langston grabbed me by my ear and dragged me to the principal's office. There I sat rubbing my arms and trying not to cry. I was hurting, but it was girls that hit me. So, I couldn't cry.

When the principal asked me what I was doing in the gym, I told him I was trying to see some panties. He thought that was funny, but not funny enough. He called my mother from her job to the school.

Now, I knew mama leaving her job was trouble. She made it perfectly clear to me after my last stomach ache that I should be near death for her to leave her job. I wasn't hurt enough for her to leave work. I tried to relay this information to the principal, but he ignored me.

Mama said very little when she got to the school. She was in her pressed white nurse's uniform and her face was stern. I saw her smile a little at the principal, but when she looked at me, the smile was gone. Walking the two blocks home, she said nothing.

When we got home, she sat me at the kitchen table and asked me if I was a pervert. I didn't know what a pervert was, but I said no because of the way she said the word. She asked what I was doing in the gym. I mumbled the truth and she told me to repeat it. I couldn't say it so she would understand. I couldn't look at my mother and tell her I was trying to see some panties. I just couldn't.

My mumbling didn't satisfy my mother, so she told me what the principal told her.

"So you want to see some panties huh? Okay little man I'm going to pull my dress up and show you some panties right now!"

I was horrified. I ran crying to my room and closed the door. I heard my mother outside my door threatening to come in and show me her panties. She kept knocking on the door telling me to come out and see some panties. She called my grandmother from next door and told her what happened. She, too, knocked on my door and asked me did I want to see her panties. When my eighth grade sister came home from school, she knocked and told me she had plenty of panties I could see. They kept this up despite my tears and pleas until my father came home from work.

I heard them tell him and I heard him laughing hard and loud. When he came in my room, he had tears in his eyes from laughing. I didn't see what was so funny. He picked me up and carried me into the kitchen were my mother, grandmother, and sister were sitting eating dinner.

He told them they better keep their clothes on and stop scaring me with their panties. And he told me that soon enough I would learn that panties were only the wrapper. Those words got him a hard smack on the butt from my mother.

Daddy had me up on his shoulders and he carried me all the way outside to the car, then we drove around the corner to the barbecue joint and got us a rib dinner. We sat in the car and ate by the junk-yard. We threw the rib bones to the junkyard dogs. Wasn't no girls and no panties in sight, just daddy, the junkyard dogs, and me.

On the way home I saw Franklin leaning against the drug store wall, staring at the locked newsstand on the corner. The day before he pointed out to me that they sold naked lady magazines at that stand, and as hard as he was staring, I knew we would be looking at the magazines soon.

3

Real Life

My name is Charity Lewis, and I am about to be a forty-eight-year-old freshman at Kennedy King Community College. This is my second time attending the school. During my first admission, I became pregnant with my daughter, Neale. I withdrew, had her, and went about the business of raising a child.

School wasn't prominent thought of mine at that time; formal education took a back seat to day-to-day life. I have always been a hardy reader. Whatever is close gets read. So my education hasn't stopped because I'm not in school. However, formal education wasn't a "priority" like the young admission clerk said a few minutes ago. Feeding my daughter and keeping a roof over our heads and clothes on both our backs were the *priorities*.

On the few occasions when returning to school was a thought, I also thought about Neale's father, Hurston. We met here. He was a nice looking young man, not real attractive, but not ugly either. Like my friend Zora said he was. She used to tease me by calling him "an ugly young buck." Hurston was ten years younger than me.

I was a twenty-eight-year-old freshman the first time I enrolled. Even though I had very good grades in high school, going to college right after graduation wasn't what was expected. I did what everyone else in my family had done and found a job. I ended up working for an industrial spool manufacturing company until my back was injured.

The county hospital doctors told me right away that I would never be able to lift anything over twenty pounds without straining my back. The doctors at the spool company didn't see it that way. My lawyers had to fight those people for eight years to get compensation, and the money they finally settled with wasn't enough to keep a kitten in catnip. But with that money, and my monthly disability check, and help from Mr. Brown, Neale and I have made it through. Now my child is going to college, and she has me going back too.

The school tried to get me to register online because I am registering late, but this mature student couldn't really follow all the prompts, so I came up here to get help. The young admissions lady has been really nice. She told me a lot of students my age have been returning to school and most of them prefer to register in person. The problem wasn't my computer literacy; the problem was confusing online directions. She smiled at me saying that and said she understood. She left with my registration card in hand and that was twenty minutes ago.

She has a nice, bight office to work in. Looks like she shares it with four other people. I see four desks with those little movable walls separating their workspace. I have never worked in an office. I imagine it would be nice work—clean and all. One young fellow has two people sitting at his desk, two young ladies, and one of them is popping gum. Lord, I wish she would stop; it sounds and looks so ignorant. A person would think that since she's trying to register for college, she would put her best foot forward. Maybe she doesn't know any better. Who knows, but I sure wish she would stop.

The truth be told, I wasn't on my best behavior the first time either. I got to Kennedy King because I sent a picture in to the Sun-Times for a contest they were having. It was for pictures of a Chicago thing or place. I took a picture of a light pole on the corner and it got an honorable mention. A photography professor from Kennedy King contacted me about a scholarship for photography students. I wasn't working, so this sister jumped at the chance to go to for school free. I came up here with the attitude that these people owed me something because they recruited me.

The only class I attended regularly was photography. I loved taking pictures almost as much I love to read. My father had given me a

Polaroid camera when I was a kid and I have always taken pictures. My daughter, Neale, draws pictures and she is good. A natural artist people say; it's because of her drawing that we are both in school.

Neale is very talented and won a scholarship to The Art Institute, but she refused to go unless I enrolled in school as well. She got the bright idea after she came across the old portfolio the professor at Kennedy King had me put together. She kept questioning me until I finally told her about the contest, the scholarship, and getting pregnant with her. Well, the child took my leaving school personal, as if she had something to do with it. I told her she was the result of a decision that she wasn't part of. My saying that didn't deter her one iota.

The next thing I knew Neale started messing around on our computer, and the child found me money for school—a scholarship for returning students and a government grant. I thanked her but said no, all that school stuff was behind me. I wouldn't have come back, if she hadn't threatened me.

Before Neale found out she had the scholarship, she had plans to go to the Army after she graduated. She hadn't enlisted, but the recruiter was on her trail. The man was calling the house daily. Neale understood perfectly well that I didn't want her in the Army. My fear for her or any woman in the service was a topic of conversation since she was a toddler. She threatened to go and forgo her scholarship unless we were both going to school. Neale is hard-headed enough to have carried out the threat, of that, I'm certain. So, the same reason I left school, got me back into school, Neale.

"Here you are, Ms. Lewis." The young lady has come back to her workspace and handed me my schedule. I like how she has her hair; those natural twist braids look so healthy. There are extensions in my braids but only until the perm grows out, then, this sister is going to go natural like my daughter and her friends.

I have registered for five classes, the same five as before: English Composition, Algebra, Physical Science, American History, and Photography. Looking at the schedule, I'm searching for the professor's name that got me here twenty years ago. I didn't think it would be there after all this time, but what catches my eye is the English teacher's name, Kaplan, H. Hurston's last name was Kaplan. Couldn't be, but to make sure I ask the young lady, "Do you know the English composition teacher's first name?"

Hurston and I met in Composition class. He was an English major, hoping to get accepted at the University of Chicago. He'd applied late, but was still hopeful. The day I was going to tell him about being pregnant was the day he found out he was accepted. He was so proud, and so looking forward to going to that school. Not wanting to be his doom cloud, nothing was said.

I was twenty-eight and he was eighteen. If the pregnancy was anybody's fault, it was mine. He deserved a chance at life without a child to slow him down. I was at college on a fluke; he was there following a plan, who was I to mess that up? So, he never knew about Neale.

"Sure Ms. Lewis, no problem, his first name is Hurston. Dr. Hurston Kaplan, he teaches here and at the University of Chicago; we're lucky to have him here. You'll like him, all the students do."

"Oh, I'm sure I will."

I leave without saying another word. Outside in my little white Corolla I ask the universe, "What are the chances of that!"

I don't even start the old car. I can't.

"What are the chances? Oh my God, Hurston? Hurston is at Kennedy King? Oh my God. This really shouldn't be happening; things have moved past this. My life, Neale's life, is past this."

I never told her that her father was dead. I told her that he left and couldn't come back, and that was good enough when she was a little girl. When she was around fourteen, I told her the truth that her father didn't know she was born and I didn't know how to find him.

She accepted that answer with no more questions. By then, a couple of her friends had gotten pregnant and she began to see how things could happen. At about sixteen she got it into her head that Mr. Brown was her daddy, in spite of the fact that I was telling her that he was just a friend of the family. "Yeah ok, if that what you two want me to think," was her reply to the truth. She had evidence, "Look, Ma. You're short; me and Mr. Brown are both tall. Ma, you are honey brown me and Mr. Brown are fudge chocolate brown. Ma, you have thick lips and kind of big ears, me and Mr. Brown have small ears and thin lips. You can say what you want Ma, but I know who my daddy is."

The two of them do favor each other enough to have some ignorant folks talking awhile back. And that little nasty, long lasting rumor only confirmed Neale's belief more. A couple of years ago she started giving him Father's Day presents and he added coal to the fire by happily taking them, "Oh that was just what I wanted baby girl." I settled with the fact that if she wanted to think he was her daddy and he didn't mind, so be it, but now her real father has surfaced.

What am I going to do? I wonder could there be more than one Hurston Kaplan in this city. It could be more than one. Before making such an assumption a sister needs to make sure. Reaching to the back seat, I grab the fall catalogue of classes. Flipping through the pages, I see that H. Kaplan is teaching an African American Literature class right now. I will just slide by and peep in, recognizing him shouldn't be a problem.

This wasn't a hot day, but suddenly I feel overheated. I don't mean to rush through the halls, but I can't help it. I have to see if it's him. Room 238 is the room: 210, 212, 218, 224, 232, there it is, 238. I take a deep breath and blow it out slow before I reach for the door, but before I could grab a hold of the knob the door is opened and standing right in front of me is Hurston. I'll be a monkey's uncle. I immediately lower my head.

"Good afternoon, are you in this class?"

"No, I'm sorry, I have you tomorrow, I registered late."

"Oh, ok, then we will see you then. I was opening the door to create breeze with the open window; it's a bit stuffy in here."

He's saying all that to my back because I am making a speedy get away. I feel his eyes on me. If I turn around, I think I would catch him staring at my butt, just like he used to do twenty years ago.

"Excuse me, Miss?"

I hear him, but I'm gone. At the stairs I take them down two at a time.

Back in my car, I start it and flee. What I'm running from, I don't know, but running is exactly what I'm doing. The question that slows me down is whether I am running from or to something - from the past or to the future? I don't know.

After I park in front of the building, I realize I am running to my daughter. I have a strong desire to see her, to be in her company, to tell her something. It's a childish feeling, like when a kid knows her teacher is going to call home and tell her mother she didn't give her the bad note from the previous week. I feel I have to tell Neale something before someone else does. But what, and where do I start?

When I enter our first floor apartment, she is typing away on the computer. The computer is in the front room of our two bedroom apartment. We both use it, so putting in her room or mine didn't seem fair, so we put in the front room and that stops both of us from over doing it. Mostly, it stops Neale from overdoing it because there is nothing on the Internet that will have me up at two in the morning like it does her. If I didn't stop the child, she would live on that thing.

"Hey, Ma."

She doesn't turn from the screen to greet me.

"Hey, baby."

"How did it go? Did you get registered?"

"Yep, without a problem."

"Get your books?"

I forgot to get the darn books!

"No, I forgot. Hey, I want you to go to classes with me tomorrow if you don't mind?"

Where that came from I don't know, but it is a good idea. I do want her to go. I want them to see each other, and once they are together, the three of us will work it out from there. This is too much for me to handle on my own; it's a three people situation. If all three of us get together, the situation will work its self out. Walking over to the computer, I bend down to kiss my baby on her cheek. She still is my baby even if she is a foot taller than me.

She looks from the screen to me, "Are you ok, Ma?" My child has always been able sense when things are not quite right with me.

"Yeah, I'm just thanking you for getting me to register for school. I think it's going to change our lives."

She shrugs her slender shoulders and goes back to typing. We both are wearing pink spaghetti strap tops. She has cut hers in half to show the whole city her flat belly. Mine is still the full length it was designed to be. Not that I couldn't wear a belly shirt, my stomach is flat, thanks to a hundred daily sit-ups. I do fifty in the morning and fifty at night. I chose not to show the whole city my stomach because I am a mother of a young adult daughter, so I dress like I have that responsibility. It looks like she is on the Art Institute's website. She is setting up some type of student account. I kiss her again and ask, "So do you think you can go to school with me tomorrow?"

"Sure Ma, I would like that, being supportive of nervous students is a good thing." She says with a smile. She has no idea how nervous I am going to be.

In my bedroom I collapse across my sleigh bed with street shoes still on. Oh how I love this bed. It was purchased because the sales clerk acted like a sister couldn't afford it, and he was right, I couldn't. But, damn if that was something he should have known. The man categorized me on the spot and that irked me beyond belief. The money that was in my bra that day was the down payment on a new used car, but it bought me the sleigh bed and respect, or so I thought.

When I came home and told Mr. Brown what happened, he laughed at me, told me I fell for a salesman's trick. He said it's the salesman goal to sell product, even if he has to anger me into buying it.

"The end result was you brought a bed with money that was earmarked for a car. So, who won, Lil Bit?"

After he laid the facts out for me, smoke was coming out of my ears. The salesman pegged me and played me. I went back up to that store and cancelled the sale and got my money back. Neale and I went and found the Corolla that afternoon. However, when I had got home, the sleigh bed was in my bedroom. Mr. Brown had brought it for me at half the price and he couldn't wait to tell me the story.

"After the salesman lost your business sell, Lil Bit, I knew he was going to be frantic as a hound to make a sale. I went in the store and fumbled around, didn't even look at beds right off and, when I did look at the beds, I looked at the real expensive ones. After awhile

I picked out a big one, cost a couple of grand. We were at the register when I had pulled out bankroll to pay for it. Teased him a little, then I told him we'd better measure the headboard because it looked too wide to for my bedroom wall.

"We measured about four other headboards until we got to the sleigh bed. Of course I told him it was the right size, but I acted like I had no interest at all. As I was walking out the door, I told him I would I buy it if he could get the price lower. We haggled over the price until he knocked half off. And that, Lil Bit, is how you got a Christmas present in July."

He still had a Christmas present for me that year, like he has for the twenty-one years I have been living in this building. One would think that the amount of time he and I have kept company that we would be a lot more serious about each other - at least living together. But that's not the case. He lives back there and I live up here. We would be a lot more serious if he wanted to be more serious.

It's funny because people think it's me stopping us from being a traditional couple, but he's the one that doesn't want to give up his freedom. He likes living back there in with his cat and his whiskey. He's set in his ways, just like his old mangy tomcat.

Him and that cat both come and go and live as they please; they're two old stubborn rascals. I tried to be friendly with the cat, but he hisses at me whenever I try to pet him. When he gets locked out, I open the door to let him in and he'll run right by as if he can't stand to be in my company. When Neale lets him in, he'll rub all against her legs and meows for her to pick him up and pet him. The mangy old tomcat is friendly with only people who he wants to be friendly with. He hisses at me and meows for Neale. He does as he pleases, the same as Mr. Brown.

Mr. Brown doesn't wash dishes until he feels like it; he doesn't get out of bed in until he's ready; he drinks as much whiskey as he wants when he wants, dresses in them old timey clothes and thinks he's sharp; gambles as much as he wants without anybody checking into his affairs, and eats as much fried pork and sardines as his blood pressure will stand.

He knows if he had a full time woman, somebody to look closely after him, all those freedoms would be gone. And when I do try to help, say, I remind him to take his medicine, he goes to fussing and carrying on as if my concern is nagging. He hisses at me just like that old tomcat, and just like I do with the tomcat, I let him be.

With me he knows all he has to do is offer a little help here and there, take me out to a play or a movie once in awhile and he will get some female company every now and then, which is how he wants it, every now and then. It's been this way since the beginning and I'm not complaining at all.

We started becoming friends a year after Neale was born. She was sick one night, constipated something terrible, and he showed me how to use a piece of soap and my fingers to get that hard booboo out of my baby.

I didn't think much about him because he was so much older. He was in his fifties then, but he kept coming around with what I needed: light bulbs, pearl earrings, milk, a winter coat, toilette paper, tennis bracelet, diapers, a oak bookcase, fresh greens, a microwave. He could fix anything that broke in the apartment or in my car. He was and is real handy to have around.

One day I asked him what he wanted from me, he said whatever I wanted to give him. I told him he was too old to be my man, he said, "I ain't tryin' to be nobody's man, I'll just help you the best I can until you can find somebody that will help you better. You, my young, tender lady friend."

To Mr. Brown, I am still a "young tender" and I like that. Over the years there have been a couple of 'somebodies' in my life, and he never interfered with my dating, but it didn't take me long to figure out that most of these men couldn't or wouldn't do half of what Mr. Brown was doing for me and Neale, especially, Neale. Anything that girl asks him to do he will do. He taught her how to ride a bike, and bought her first bike. He taught her how to drive, and bought her first vehicle, and when one of the local thugs was harassing her, it was him who whispered something in the boys ear that got him out of her life. He is not her biological father, but she's right,

Mr. Brown is her daddy. Last week he showed me his insurance papers and she is listed as a beneficiary along with his legal children, none of his past wives or me were listed.

Me not being listed didn't upset me, what angered me was that two of those kids on the list were younger than Neale. I was a little salty behind that, it was bad enough not being listed, but the two younger kids got me to seeing red. He had gotten some woman pregnant after he and I became friends.

I kick my shoes off and swing my feet up on the bed. My mind is filled and starting to spin a little, jumping from situation to situation and person to person . . . Mr. Brown's kids . . . school . . . Hurston . . . Neale. How did I forget to buy my books? Running away from the Hurston situation is how.

Hurston looked good; still slim and a full head of hair, He was wearing glasses, but they added "character" as Neale would say. That's what she said about my few gray hairs, "They add character Ma, don't color them."

Sitting up, I look into the bureau mirror. There are only a few gray hairs, and if they weren't all clumped together at the front of my head. They would probably go unnoticed.

I have no wrinkles or laugh lines to speak of, only a little pudge under my chin. No bags under my eyes, at least not today. Overall, I am still a good-looking sister. With these extended cornrows, more than one young man has run up on me about to rap until they see I am a grown woman or a "vet" like I heard one of them say walking away, "Man she's a vet, but she got a nice booty."

My butt is still firm and standing, can't say that for my breasts. They went south years ago. But the booty is still holding its own. It held Hurston's eyes.

Hurston.

Husrton and Neale.

I get out of the bed, walk over to the window, and look out for Mr. Brown's black Cadillac. It's there. He is parked behind me. I slide into my house shoes, which use to be Mr. Brown's house shoes and walk up front to the door.

"Where you going, Ma?" comes from Neale who is now in the kitchen at the refrigerator. The girl is all legs and those cut off blue jean short's she wearing are way too short for my comfort. Instead of arguing with her about them now, I'll just lose them at the laundromat later.

"Over to Mr. Brown's."

"Be sure to tell him about the my Blazer pulling to the left, and the Men's Day celebration at church; remind him that he promised to attend because you know he's going to try to get out of it." She says with a smile.

Neale joined church all on her own. I'm proud of her for that. Despite my CME attendance(Christmas, Mothers Day and Easter) Neale has become a regular member. I just wish she dressed more like a church girl.

"Will do, baby," I say going out the door.

There are three apartments on the first floor of our building— mine, Zora's and Mr. Brown. Mr. Brown's, who has lived here longer than Zora, or me, is at the end of the hall. His apartment was por- tioned off from the one that Zora rents. My mother told me at one time that all these old brownstones were small mansions, but during World War II people sliced them up to make room for renters.

Mr. Brown lives in a kitchenette. I should say lived in a kitchenette because the old man is seldom home these days. His absence really shouldn't matter because I have had very little to say to him since I saw those younger kids listed on the insurance papers. But I do need to talk to him now, to get his advice on the Hurston situation and hear what he thinks about me taking Neale up to the school tomorrow. He advice is always so sound, so matter of fact.

I knock on his door and push it open all at the same time.

He is sitting in his rust colored reclining chair with that mangy gray tomcat in his lap. He hears me enter and smiles at me when I come in. The tomcat hisses - it is an ugly old thing.

"Hey, college girl" he grins. He thought Neale bullying me into going back to school was real funny. We laughed about it for a good while, but that was before I found out about the younger kids.

What Mr. Brown tries to do is only talk about pleasant stuff and not his mess. He tries to get me laughing when I should be angry. Usually, I go along with him, but a sister needs to know about those darn kids. My intentions were not to come back here to bring that up; the needed conversation is about Hurston and Neale, but seeing him sitting there rubbing that "live as he pleases" tomcat has made me mad. Along with the fact that he's wearing those maroon and grey-checkered polyester pants with those grey lace up Stacy Adam shoes, and a shiny maroon nylon shirt. He insists on wearing those out-of-style clothes even after me and Neale bought him much better clothing. His closet is filled with new jeans, dress pants, and shirts from past Christmases, birthdays and Fathers' Days, but he won't wear them unless we insist. He'd rather wear those played-out fashions. Large retail stores don't even sell those type of pants, shirts or shoes. He has to drive all the way out to Harvey to buy those old-timey clothes and the man who owns the store is just a old and stubborn as he is. It's crazy; an old-timey clothes store filled with old men buying discontinued fashions like they're shopping at a boutique on Michigan Avenue.

I am standing here, staring hard at Mr. Brown and that cat, searching my mind for the right words. I didn't come back to talk about those kids. I need his advice and this is not the time to argue.

"Lil Bit, why is you standing there like somebody done snatched a hold of your bloomers. What ails you?"

"You ail me!" The tone is nasty even to my ears.

"Huh?"

"You and those kids born after Neale. Where did those kids come from?" It's a direct question, but I will bet a fifty dollar bill to a doughnut that I won't get a direct answer.

"A grown woman like you knows where babies come from, don't you?"

He's grinning big now. Showing his top silver tooth and his bottom gold one. Only a truly ignorant person would mix gold and silver teeth.

"Don't play with me, Mr. Brown."

"Lil Bit, I showed you them insurance papers to make you happy, not to get you all riled up."

"Well, I am riled up, and I want to know where them kids younger than Neale came from! And where the hell you been sleeping, cause you ain't slept back here in a week!"

This is not how Mr. Brown and I talk to each other. The tone is the one that comes out when I am angry with Neale. I hear my foot tapping on his linoleum floor and my arms have crossed across my chest. I should have taken off my starched white cotton button-down shirt before I laid on the bed. I could have gotten another wear out of it, but now the arms are wrinkled.

"Girl, what got stuck in your craw and sent you back here madder than a wet hen?"

"I have told you what's bothering me Mr. Brown, them kids and where you been."

He looks at me with half a grin on his face and says, "Lil Bit, them is my grandkids."

"What?"

"My grandkids, Lil Bit. I got two grandbabies," He says still grinning while petting that darn cat.

"But they got your last name?"

"My daughter ain't married; she is too evil a woman to keep a man." Now he's looking at me like he just said something clever, trying to call me evil on the sly.

"Well, where you been sleeping? Cause you sure haven't been sleeping back here."

"Lil Bit, I wanted to tell you this in my own time, but looks like it's got to be your time. I have prostate cancer. I been staying over night at the VA because of the chemo treatments. The only time they could fit me in was late at night. Since the treatment drains my strength, they arranged for me to stay overnight."

He's looking at me hard, trying to read my thoughts. He thinks he can do that. The grin has left his face but a slight smile is lingering, he says, "When you get to acting jealous?"

I'm not acting jealous, a sister was understandably curious about where her friend had been.

"Ain't nobody jealous of your old self." I say pulling the chair from the kitchen table to the side of his recliner. "How is the treatment going?" I am looking around at the off-white walls trying not to look into his face. I have known no one who has gotten better from cancer. Sure you hear stories about miraculous recoveries, but I personally know no one who has survived and this takes my anger for Mr. Brown away.

"Aw, it didn't do so good." He sighs and runs his finger across his shaved head. He sighs again. "They told me today they think the cancer has spread, so, they stopped the treatment."

He looks at me straight on. The whites around his brown eyes are strained and red. He is tired.

"Hey, you know I am glad you came back here Lil Bit, I want to give you something." From the end table on the other side of the chair he picks up a folder, "This is the deed to this building. It has been willed to you."

The radiation from the chemo treatment must be getting to him. He doesn't own this building.

"You don't own this building, Mr. Brown."

"Who owns it then?"

"The Brown Realty Group?"

"Lil Bit, I am the Brown Realty Group." He's grinning again.

"Mr. Brown, maybe you should pull out the bed and stretch out a bit. Want me to pull it out of the wall for you?"

I have heard about the radiation messing with folks minds, but I thought that was after awhile.

"How long have you been taking the chemo treatments, Mr. Brown?"

"Off and on? Oh, a good number of years, yes a good number, the cancer started in my spleen, but they thought they had got it all. Now it is in my prostrate and they think it's in my kidneys.

"I got to be honest with you, all this testing and treatment along with my pressure, got me feeling kinda of slow. I'm glad they got me going in the hospital today, allow me to get some rest and build up a little strength. I don't like feeling this weak. Open the folder like I told you."

He doesn't look as sick as he says he is. Yes, I have noticed a little ash on his normally healthy dark skin, but I thought that was from him halfway taking care of himself. I didn't think he was sick. Mr. Brown doesn't get sick, no more than his blood pressure. He has never mentioned cancer before. I reach over and grab his hand. The cat, who can't stand to be near me, hisses and jumps out of Mr. Brown's lap to the floor, then up on the white iron sink and out the kitchen window.

I hold Mr. Brown's one hand with my two. His hand looks older than the man I know he is. This hand doesn't look like it can turn a wrench, drive a nail with a hammer, paint a bathroom, wash my car, tote my duffel bags to the laundry, or squeeze butt just hard enough to make me want to do it. Mr. Brown's hand can do all that. This hand looks like an old man's hands, not my Mr. Brown's hand. My Mr. Brown doesn't get sick; he eats what he wants; he drinks when he wants, and doesn't get sick. This is an old man's hand.

"Don't cry, Lil Bit. Stop that, it's not as bad as all that."

I don't like crying. I don't like when my body does something I didn't know it was going to do. With his other hand, Mr. Brown is wiping the tears from my cheeks.

"When you go in that hospital, you better do exactly what they tell you. Don't be having Neale bring sardines, pig's feet, and all the kind of stuff up there. You got to get better. Neale needs you to fix the raggedy Blazer you bought her and she expecting you to go to Men's Day program in a couple of weeks, so you can't be messing around at that hospital. Go on in there and come right out."

I am crying too hard now. I have to leave. I stand, "I will see you later, Mr. Brown. What Hospital?"

"I'll be out at the VA in Maywood. Here, take the folder with you."

He puts the folder in my hand as I turn to leave. I turn back around and kiss him. I kiss him hard and long. I want him to know that I care about him.

"You get better, Mr. Brown, you get better quick." I feel his hand squeezing my butt.

"Lil Bit, it's nothing but tests, not worry yourself like this."

"Ok," I answer, but I know better. Mr. Brown is sick. I pull his door closed behind me head down the hall to Zora's.

I knock four times on her door before she opens it. She has a new man, and, when she has a new man, she tries to wear him out before they break up. Zora has had over eight men living with her, and that's just been at this building. I know she lived with a couple after we graduated out of high school and she lived with that white man on the north side while I was pregnant with Neale. In reality, I truly have no idea how many men Zora has really lived with, I could only guess.

None of the other women in the building or on the block have much to say to her, but they have plenty to say about her. Not to me because they know Zora is my friend and I spit fire when people mess with mine. The door opens, Zora is gathering her robe and I can smell the sex.

"Girl, get dressed and come on out on the porch, I need to talk."

"Ok, give me a minute, Charity."

"Don't have me sitting out there waiting if you ain't coming tell me."

"I said I'm coming! Damn." She looks like she was having a good time up until I started knocking at her door and messed it up. For some reason interrupting her groove has me feeling a little better. She closes her door and I snicker.

Our building has a small porch but you would think it was a wrap around because of all the people that sit out here. However, this afternoon it's only me out here. The block isn't that busy either. The only folks out here is the mailman at the other end and little Joy across the street. She is behind the chain link fence that surrounds her grand-mama's yard. She's playing with the dolls Neale gave her last week.

Neale got tired of seeing Joy playing with stick people for dolls and gave her old doll collection to her. Joy's ornery old grandmother didn't say a word of thanks. She is still mad about her daughter being on drugs. She acts like it's the whole neighborhood's fault, so she has nothing pleasant to say to anyone. But she was the one that kept the girl locked up in the house and when she came outside, she had to stay behind the same fence little Joy is behind.

When Joy's mother got the freedom of catching the bus to high school, the girl went wild and started hanging with a crowd of fast girls. One thing led to another, and now she's out there, messed up bad with drugs. I believe kids need to know their surroundings. That way they know the dangers, know what and who to avoid. The girl had no experience prior to high school.

Neale wasn't allowed to run the streets, but she was allowed to outside the yard and off the porch. She became friends with the other kids in the neighborhood. She went to block parties, high school games, and all that type of stuff. I even let her go to a couple of house parties if I knew something about the parents. Kids need freedom to grow. Joy's grandmother didn't let her mother have that freedom and it doesn't look like Joy is going to get it either.

There is a little overcast now and a cool breeze blowing through. We might get a little rain; the grass needs it. I walk to the edge of the porch and sit down, knowing the concrete is going to leave dust on my black jeans, but I don't care.

Parked in front of our building are Neale's Blazer, my Corolla, and Mr. Brown's Cadillac. Zora sold the used BMW she bought. She took in for brake work and found out the maintenance costs were beyond her means. I didn't think she needed a car anyway. She is darn near blind and refuses to wear glasses or contacts. She's too vain for glasses and says the contacts irritate her eyes. She works right around the corner. Zora's sister owns a popular bar, which she manages, and that's why she can keep a constant flow of men in her life. She works at a party and people are always telling her about places and events to go. She is always around men, so she meets a lot of them. This is added to the fact that she is "drop dead gorgeous," as Mr. Brown says, doesn't hurt her prospects one bit.

I asked him one day why he had chose to spend time with me when Zora was so attractive to him. Oh, she used to flirt with him until she found out we were friends. Once she knew he and I were keeping company, all her flirting stopped. I like that about her. I have never known her to mess with anybody's husband or boyfriend.

What Mr. Brown said about her was, "Yeah, she is a fine, ain't no doubt, but I don't think she makes a good friend to a man. You and me is friends, Lil Bit. Zora ain't go be no man's friend. She wants too much from them to be friends, and she don't give a man a chance to be her friend. Always telling men what they got to do to be with her. Men like to do without being told. If a man won't or can't do for her, she ain't go be bothered with him. A woman who is always asking, don't get gifts, she gets paid. And I don't like friends I have to pay." He came real close to calling her a whore, but stopped a bit shy of it.

I never have to ask Zora about her many men friends because she likes talking about them. Her stories can be better than cable T.V. sometimes. Over the years, however, I have noticed a pattern to her relationships and now realize that she doesn't want to keep a man. She likes having new men every so often. When I told her that, she only laughed and said, "Lust is better than love." I think that's a very sad way to live a life, but I didn't tell her that.

"What's so important that you have knock on my door like you're the police? And don't say a thing about me smoking these cigarettes; it's a package deal. If you want to talk to me, you have to breathe through some cigarette smoke because I'm going to smoke me a couple of these while I'm out here because Phillip doesn't smoke.

"You know he is my personal trainer right? Girl, the muscles! I have never had a man with such stamina and he's fifty. Fifty-years old and doing like he's nineteen. Ok, not nineteen because there aren't too many repeat performances. But the one nightly show has got me applauding. You know what I mean right?"

She has slipped into a nice tan sundress and a pair of white flip-flops. I think I bought the sundress for her birthday last year. She pulling hard on one of her Virginia Slims and looking down at me; she blows the smoke up in the air.

"The dress looks nice on you, Vanny."

"You think? Phillip said that too." She sits next to me on the edge of the porch, pack of cigarettes and lighter in one hand, two fingers scissoring a Virginia Slim in the other.

"That's right, you registered for school today didn't you? How did it go? Did something happen up there? Is that why you need to talk? Are you getting scared? Charity, you can do the school thing. You know that."

To me, Zora looks like I imagined Cleopatra—tall, dark, and regal. She has a slim build, narrow facial features and a keen nose.

"Yes, something happened at school, but it's something else too. Mr. Brown is going into the hospital. He's sick."

"How sick?"

"Cancer sick."

"Oh, shit. Damn." She flicks the lit cigarette all the way out into the street. A yellow taxi runs over it and stops.

"Does Neale know?"

"He just told me."

"Damn. I'm sorry, Charity."

"I'm certain he's going to be all right. It just threw me for a loop that he's sick. I mean, I knew about the blood pressure, but cancer is so much more serious."

The taxi has parked in front of Joy's yard.

"It is serious, but people get through it. My mother and sister survived breast cancer."

"I didn't know they had cancer, Zora. I remember when you went down South to help your mother—about five years ago right?"

Getting out of the cab is Joy's mother and a man.

"Yeah, that was the trip. I stayed way longer than I planned, but things turned out for the best. She's doing fine now. My sister's episode was two years ago; she fared better than my mother, she didn't lose a breast."

Watching her light another cigarette I ask, "Ain't you scared to smoke, knowing it's in your family?"

The man getting out of the cab is dressed in a forest green business suit and Joy's mother is in a black skirt and yellow blouse, and she is wearing heels. The last time I saw her, her hair was going every which away and her clothes wear dirty and worn. Today her hair is in a bun and she's neat as a pin. She looks better than I have seen her look in years.

"I try not to think about cancer, Charity. I'll stop smoking when I'm ready. Is that little Joy's mama going in the yard? It must be, look how excited Joy is. Don't the mama look good! And got a clean-cut man with her. I wonder what's going on over there. Look, she still got her key, that's good. The evil old woman didn't take her house key from her." She exhales and pulls more smoke into her, "I hope Mr. Brown has health insurance."

"He's a veteran. He's getting treated at the VA."

"That's good news. Cancer treatment can eat away at man's fortune. As wealthy as Mr. Brown is, hospital bills can still break him."

"What makes you think Mr. Brown is wealthy?"

"What do you mean? The man owns Brown Realty. He'd better be wealthy. I know for a fact he owns this building, the one next door, the one on the corner, and the building my sister's bar is in. People say he has property in the Loop, but I don't know how true that is. But you know all this don't you?"

I don't answer because I didn't know it.

"Girl, don't tell me you didn't know. You are not that naïve or innocent. Are you?" She's looking at me hard. "Girl, you didn't know! Then why were you bothering with that old man?"

"Mr. Brown ain't that old Zora. And we have been friends a long time. He is my friend, so I didn't have to have a reason to be bothered with him! God, Zora, is everything so black and white for you?"

I look away from her because I feel tears coming.

"Charity, I wasn't trying to get you all upset and on your high horse. I just assumed you knew the man was rich."

"I have never asked Mr. Brown about his money, I thought he worked on those buildings to help out with a social security check or something. His money is his affair."

Zora blows out a big puff of smoke and it lingers around our heads. I fan it apart.

"Sorry," she says.

Looking down at the folder in my hand, I understand what Mr. Brown is doing. It is the same with the insurance papers; he doesn't think he's going to make it.

"I don't want him to be sick, Zora. He means so much to Neale. What will she do if something happens to him? Mr. Brown is her Daddy as far as she is concerned."

"She's going to do the same as you and keep living. When my daddy died, I shut down for a while because I loved that man, Charity. We all did—my mama, my sister and me. He made our lives wonderful; we never wanted for a thing when he was alive. He treated us like a queen and two princesses. The man my mother married after my daddy wasn't half the man he was. We lived in a house half the size and had half the things. I got over my daddy's death and got on with my life, which is what people do who love life and you and Neale love life."

Darn it, the tears are falling again. "I just want Mr. Brown to be ok."

"That's up to the God, you know that, Charity."

"Yeah, you right, but knowing that doesn't make it any easier for me. I'm still gonna worry."

Zora is taking another long pull on her cigarette, but stops midway and points across the street, "Girl, look over across the street!"

Joy's mama has her in her arms and the man in the green suit is lugging out a chest. The waiting cab opens the trunk and the man in the suit and the cab driver load the chest into the car. Little Joy has one of Neale's dolls in her hand. They all pile into the cab, no sign of the grandmother. As the cab is pulling off, little Joy waves goodbye out of the back window. We wave back.

"A chest ain't a suitcase. You think the mama got her life together good enough to come get her child?"

"I hope so Zora, I really do."

We both stand and watch the cab drive down the block and turn onto 47th Street.

"Hey, you want to ride up to the bookstore with me? I forgot to get my books earlier. I could use the company."

"Girl, I would, but Phillip had oral surgery this afternoon and he wants me to go with him. Get Neale to go with you, that way you can tell her about, Mr. Brown."

"It's more than Mr. Brown that I have to tell Neale about. You remember Hurston, her real daddy?"

"Girl, you ain't said that name in years. What makes you speak it now?" She sits back down on the porch and I follow.

"I saw him up at the school; matter of fact, he's going to be my English teacher."

"You lying!"

"I wish I was." I watch her pull yet another cigarette from the pack and light it. She must have finished off the other one when I was looking at little Joy.

"Girl, you got all types of messes around you; no wonder you need to talk. So, what's up with Hurston? Did y'all reminisce some?" She twists and pumps her hips while sitting, "He's a grown man now, you wouldn't be robbing the cradle." She says with a wink and an exhale.

"Shut up, I wasn't robbing the cradle then, he was eighteen. We were both young." I say in my own defense.

"Wrong, he was a minor and you was grown. The boy was fresh out of high school when you nabbed him."

"You make it sound a lot nastier than it was."

"How? You was damn near thirty and he was just out of high school. That's the way it was. You grabbed a hold of the young ugly buck and rode him good until he popped one too many inside you. Now that's what happened."

She inhales again and then flicks the less than half smoked cigarette into the street.

"That's not how it was and you know it. We had something real for a little while."

"I'm not saying y'all didn't, but you robbed the cradle to get it. So what happened, did y'all talk?"

I didn't rob the cradle, Hurston was the aggressor in the relationship; he pursued me and Zora knows it. I gave him my number because I thought it was cute that he asked me, I didn't think anything real was going to happen, but one conversation led to another and the next thing I knew, we were dating.

"No, I ran away like a school girl. But tomorrow I have to face him; he's my English teacher."

"What are you going to tell Neale?"

'My plan is to take her up to school with me, get them in the same room, and go from there."

A sly smirk crosses her face, "I'm going too. You might need some back up." She was asking and telling me at the same time.

"You going to be nosey."

"True, but you still might need some back up."

"You right, Lord only knows how Neale will respond."

"When you gonna tell her about Mr. Brown?"

"After school, we will all ride out to the VA hospital to see him."

"If Neale will go anywhere with you after you drop the daddy bomb on her."

She's has a point. There are a million and one ways Neale could respond and I am not about to wrack my brain trying to figure out what she will do.

"I'm going in to take a nap, been moving since six this morning." I stand and stretch and Zora does the same.

"What time do we leave in the morning?"

"Seven and don't be late."

"I won't be, please believe. This drama I would pay to see."

"He did look good."

"Who? Hurston?" She says in disbelief.

"Yes, Hurston. He is still slim and a head full of hair, his face remains hairless, it doesn't look like he aged much."

"Well, you met him when he was baby."

"Unh, I'm too through with you. See you in the morning."

"Ok, girl, you go on in I'm going to smoke one more before I go in." She pulls one from the pack and lights up as the door closes behind me.

Entering the apartment, I hear the shower running. Neale is getting ready to go skating. Her boyfriend is a skate guard at a rink out in Maywood. When he has to work, she goes with him. A cheap date I call it. The young boy is pleasant enough and polite. He's in his third year at Chicago State University. His people are from the West Side; his mother is a bus driver and daddy, a disc jockey. I have actually been to a couple of his daddy's steppers sets. He's much better looking than his daddy. He should thank his mama for that.

I close the bedroom door behind me, and fall across my bed. The clock reads one thirty. It's been a heck of a morning and afternoon. I should get up and put those chicken breasts in the crock pot. I don't. What I really should do is drive Mr. Brown out to the VA hospital to find out what's going on with him.

I stand up with that on my mind and go to the window to make sure his Cadillac is still outside. I see a Medi-car and Mr. Brown climbing into the side door. He has arranged is transportation. Mr. Brown takes care of his business; he always has. The folder he gave me is on the bed. I pick it up and open it. It's a deed, at least it looks like a deed to me, behind the document is a letter written to me in Mr. Brown's writing.

He says he wishes he could have left me more, but with three ex-wives, nine children and five grand children, he had to spread the pie kind of thin. He is also leaving the Cadillac to me, along with the care of the tomcat. He tells me he loves me and to take care of Neale because he loves her too.

Mr. Brown isn't expecting to come home from the hospital. I cry myself to sleep.

I have a crazy dream; it's not a dream, but rather, it's more like a memory. I am reliving every date Hurston and I had. The first one was at Gino's East, the second to the show at Evergreen Plaza, and then to the various hotel rooms we rented across the South Side. The crazy part is that on every date, I am wearing red and somehow Mr. Brown shows up right before we kiss or get sexual. I didn't even know Mr. Brown back then. We didn't move into the building until Neale was a month old. And I never wore red until after meeting Mr. Brown. The color was too bold for me, but since he loves me in red, I began to wear it.

When I wake up, the clock reads six thirty and the shower is still running. Neale must have left the water on. I burst into the bathroom to see that Neale is in the shower, but she has her morning toiletries on the sink, mouthwash, toothpaste etc. I leave the bathroom without disturbing her, the computer clock read six thirty-five. Oh my God, I have sleep a whole day away.

At my closet I don't have a clue as to what to wear; something not too sexy, not too matronly, not too business, not too young, not too old, not too serious and not too playful. I settle with white jeans, a red chiffon top, and red snakeskin sandals.

While I'm in the shower, the doorbell rings. It slipped my mind to tell Neale that Zora was going to the school with us, drying off I hear them laughing and talking. I wave to Zora while making it to bedroom. She says something about going to get breakfast sandwiches; I order the sausage, egg, and cheese one.

Once dressed, I get on my knees and say a needed prayer for guidance and Mr. Brown's health. We all load into Neale's Blazer for comfort; they both had complained about the tightness of the Corolla.

I sit in the back of the Blazer and eat my breakfast sandwich without saying a word. They don't notice because Zora and Neale enjoy each other's company immensely. They both love music, R&B being their shared favorite. Zora loves jazz and she feels it's her duty to pass her knowledge of the music on to Neale. In return Neale who loves rap updates Zora on hip hop. They exchange CDs and the reporting back and forth to each other and can go on for hours— which is what they are doing now. It appears Zora gave Neale a Monk CD, and Neale gave her a Missy Elliot CD. And both appeared to have enjoyed the exchange.

My mind is on Hurston. What will he think of me? I will be his student. Will he think I have been lazy over the years, not having a degree? Will he look at me as a failure? I have often thought of myself as one. All I have done with my life is raise Neale. Other women have done that and a lot more. His wife probably has. She's probably a college professor too. What am I besides Mr. Brown's tender young thing and Neale's mama? Hurston is a University of Chicago Professor; me, I'm just a woman he got pregnant. I can't do this. Not today.

Today, I need to be Mr. Brown's young tender thing and nothing else. I need to be that because Mr. Brown needs me. The man I am something too needs me. My man needs me. What I'm thinking? I need to be at that hospital.

"Mama?" Neale's eyes are on mine in the rearview mirror. She's driving, her and Zora are up front. "You're crying, what's wrong?"

There is no sense in not telling her.

"Baby, the man teaching the my English class is your biological father. My plan was to have you two meet today. But something more important has happened. I found out yesterday that your daddy, Mr. Brown, is dying of cancer. And baby, I would much rather go see him today, than go through this mess up at the school. Don't get me wrong, it's important for you to meet your father and believe me you are going to meet Mr. Hurston Kaplan, just not today. I think we should spend this day with your daddy. If you don't mind, baby?"

"Mr. Brown is dying? I knew something was wrong, mama. I felt it all inside of me. When I saw you this morning, Zora, I thought it was something wrong with you. Mr. Brown don't get sick, Mama; you must have got it wrong. Let's go up to the hospital and get it right. You got it wrong, mama. Mr. Brown ain't sick."

"What about the school?" Zora asks.

"We can deal with that later. I need to see about my daddy."

"Your daddy's at the West Side VA hospital. Get on the expressway and I'll direct you from there. Do you want me to drive?"

"No, it's pulling a little to the left. My daddy has to fix it before I let anybody else drive it. He showed me how accommodate for the pulling when it happened on the other side. It won't take him long to fix it, you know how fast he fixes things mama."

At the doorway of his room we three are standing waiting for a technician to pull some type of machine from his room. When the tech and the machine exit, we walk in. Mr. Brown's eyes are closed. He's sitting up, propped erect with pillows.

"Hey, Mr. Brown." Neale says pushing past Zora and me to get to him. Mr. Brown opens his eyes and turns his head to face us.

"Hey, Neale, girl! How you get way out here?" His voice is barely above a whisper, but his smile is big. For some reason, after all these years, I actually like how his top gold tooth looks with the bottom silver one. Neale bends down to kiss him on the cheek and forehead.

"Who is that behind you? You brought your mama and Zora out here." His eyes are smiling with him. "Lil Bit, didn't you have school today?"

"I start next week. I only registered this week."

He looks at me with narrowing eyes. "Mmph, I thought you was registering late and classes started this week."

"Well, you just thought wrong," I say bending down kissing his other cheek, "you don't know everything." He's slipped his hand around to grab a hold of my butt and he has a nice grip on it too.

"Lil Bit, gal, I loves you and Neale."

"We know Mr. Brown," Neale says, "and we love you too."

"I ain't leaving you out, Zora, but these here my girls. I will love them to the end. I had to take small steps with Lil Bit to get her, took me the better part of ten years. You looking good in that red, Ms. Charity Lewis, I told you that is your color." The smile fades from his face as he nods asleep. He head raises and he says, "You know it must have been some strong stuff in that shot they gave me cause I'm getting kinda of tired.

"Lil Bit, these people out here is crazy. They sent in a man nurse to wash me up this morning and I was suppose to let him wash my privates. Shoot, I ain't that sick. Before you leave, Lil Bit, I want you to help me wash up some."

His head lowers again, but he wakes up before it goes all the way down.

"It's good to have folks around that care about me. Some people leave here with nobody they love close. That's not gonna happen to me now because y'all here. Well, will you look over there. How did ya'll get my old tomcat past that mean nurse?"

We turn to look but none of us see the cat.

"That ole mean nurse wouldn't even bring me any Jello, and, Neale, you done snuck my cat past her. I'ma have to watch you girl, you getting slick. Come here, boy, ain't he fine? This old gray cat been my friend for over twelve years now. Hold on, boy, don't leave, let me get you some sardines."

I feel his grip release my butt and I hear him exhale such a large breath that I don't want to look down at him. He's gone and I know it.

The monitor beeps continuously and the room is flooded with hospital staff. There is nothing they can do. Neale and Zora know it too. We hold each other's hands and leave the hospital together.

In the Blazer Neale says, "He was a real good man, mama, and a real good daddy. I will never have another daddy. I don't need one, you understand me."

I understand she's hurt, that's what I understand. After awhile she will want to meet Hurston Kaplan, so tomorrow in class I will reintroduce myself to him. I will tell him about his daughter. We will take small steps, as Mr. Brown suggested.

"Baby, that's fine. Baby, that's fine."

4

The Mailman's Cherry Grove Blues

What? What's that you say? Yes, I'm sure. I am finished with the detective business. The train doesn't have to hit me to get me off the tracks. Yeah, I know I said it would be easy work and it was. I solved the case. I figured it out as easily as I do all the mystery movies and novels. The real life mysteries, they have consequences once they end. Consequences I don't want to be part of.

What am I going to do next? Well, you know I still have my postal pension and that poor girl did pay me my fee, despite the outcome. I plan to do what I should have done from the beginning of my retirement—help my brother run the laundromat we bought last year.

Working in a laundromat is the speed an old fella like me should be moving. I will be checking on washers and dryers instead of murderers. I was wrong; being proficient at solving movie plots does not qualify one to solve crimes. I stand corrected. Don't worry, I'll be sticking to the movie plots from now on.

Yes, it was a good thing I figured it out. I'm not selling the deed short. What I'm saying is that this line of work is not for me. There is too much time on your feet in the detective business. I spent more time walking behind folks than I did driving behind them, and sometimes I ran to keep up. No, this is not the line of work for a retired mail carrier. I spent my time on my feet. The laundromat is more my speed, tinkering on a machine instead of chasing a fiend. Yes, the murderer was a fiend. Make no mistake about it, only a fiend is that hateful.

In fact, that's where the police went wrong, not seeing all of the hate in the act. They only looked at the occurrence of the murder. I knew there was more to it when I noticed every strand of hair missing from the boy's body. Everyone else was stuck on his dreadlocks being removed and I was too for a moment. When they let me see the autopsy photos, the boy being hairless stuck with me.

No, it wasn't the police that got me involved; it was the boy's girlfriend. Neither Old Sheriff nor the university police wanted me to see the boy's autopsy photos, but his girlfriend studies law at the university. She made them release the photos. The boy had been dead for six months before she called me in on the case.

She was upset because Old Sheriff really didn't look into the boy's case the way she thought he should have. You're right; she didn't try to hide the fact that she didn't care for the local folks, but she cared about that boy. She didn't care who she rubbed the wrong way. She wanted his murderer found. Well, that was before I actually found the murderer. After the murderer was identified, she felt different about the whole situation.

Yes, you're right. I showed her that small-town-born doesn't necessarily mean a small brain. What . . . my first clue? You've been watching too many movies. There really are no clues; things simply hook up. You're right again. "Simply" is not the correct word, because there was nothing simple about the event.

I guess you could say the boy being hairless was my first clue. No, that's not right. My first clue was the boy himself. He was odd to me. I'd never seen a white person with dreadlocks until his girlfriend showed me the picture they took a week before he died.

I think dreadlocks are strange on my own people, so seeing them on that young white boy set me back a step. What? No, I'm not lying. They had grown half way down his back. I wish I still had his picture, but his girlfriend took all her stuff back.

The police were certain his death was attributed to his dreadlocks. When they found him, he'd been scalped. That's why I say the police didn't look past the event of the murder. If they would have really looked at the boy, they would have seen his whole body was hairless, but all they saw was his missing dreadlocks. They didn't report that in the newspapers. They tried to keep it quiet. They didn't want his death associated with a hate crime.

I don't know much about the significance of having dreadlocks, but the police knew less than me. Some of them thought the dreadlocks meant he was gay; others thought they meant he was half black. Either way, it added up to a hate crime for them, and they wanted to keep it as quiet as possible.

I didn't expect too much help from either the university or city police department, but I got tell you at least Old Sheriff didn't get in my way. Those darn university cops tried to stop me at every pass. Most of the actual investigation was done on campus, so I saw them almost daily.

I am certain that one of them is extremely prejudiced. Yes, the thin one with the black hair. He called me an "old nigger" under his breath on more than one occasion. He said it loud enough for only me to hear. He was trying to provoke me in front of others. I played him cool. He was not the first ignorant man to call me a nigger, and I doubt he'll be the last.

What? Yeah, he's the one whose basement flooded two weeks ago and Jr. still hasn't gone out there to see about it. What? You shouldn't say things that you don't know are true. I have nothing to do with how my son runs his plumbing business. Besides, there are plenty of plumbers his skinny prejudice behind can call up from the city. I hear tell they will come up here and do work for three times what Jr. charges. A lot of folks like him have to pay that rate. Prejudice costs.

What? No, the young boy's body wasn't found on campus. Don't you remember? They found him down the road from Cornliquor's place. Remember?

Cornliquor closed his shop for the first time in twenty years. There were too many police cars out there for him: Old Sheriff's two, three from the universities, the three or so from the county, and the five or six from the state. Seeing all those squad cars almost took Cornliquor to his maker that morning.

Old Sheriff said he had to catch him before he drove back down to the river and blew up his still. You know Old Sheriff wasn't going to have that, not as much as he likes Cornliquor's hooch. Anyway, they found that poor boy in a shallow grave in the cherry grove. You remember now don't you? Yeah, I knew you would.

Yep, they found him in the cherry grove. It was sad, but I'm going to be honest with you—it made me angry. I was pissed off because one of the university kids knew about our cherry grove. I didn't want those kids in our grove. They're all over our town changing everything. Tell me when was the last time you was able to watch a game at Ron's Bar? The cherry grove was the only place left were none of them came. It was still ours. That was until he died in it. Now, it too has the university stamp on it.

You know, in a way, I got the university stamp on me too. It was the major increase in mail that came with the university that forced me to retire. I could have worked another five years with my old route. I couldn't handle the increase. You know my route takes three mail carriers now. Yes sir, the university sure has changed things around here.

Once I made up my mind to retire, I sort of put the murder out of my mind. It wasn't until the boy's girlfriend walked through my door did I give him another thought. She was my first and last client. She was all business from the first day. She came through my office door with her own investigative plan.

What? Yeah, I followed her plan after we made some changes. She had good ideas and she was providing the money. Huh? No, I wouldn't say she was my partner. I'd say she had a lot of input. For example, it was her idea to talk to his friends. Of course I would have thought of that, but she had already prepared a list complete with dorm room numbers. I followed her plan, but I wouldn't have called her my partner. She was not part of my actual investigation.

Now, I'm telling you after seeing the boy's friends from a distance, I thought his girlfriend was stringing me along. Why? Because each one of his friends was baldheaded. He was a white boy with dreadlocks; why would his friends look like . . . uh . . . what do you call them . . . uh . . . skinheads?

I watched them for two days before I actually approached them. If they were what they looked like, I wanted to be brief and to the point. The second day revealed that they weren't skinheads at all, at least not like the ones I'd heard about. Two of these young fellows appeared to have black girlfriends.

Well, after I talked to them I found out that they were a reggae band; all of them black girls were in it too. Now this was the kicker— up until a month ago they all had dreadlocks. I sat there at the cafeteria table and tried to imagine those four white boys with dreadlocks. I couldn't do it; but the black girls assured me it was true.

The baldheaded boys told me that a month ago all their hair fell out and not just from their heads but their entire bodies. They were all completely hairless, except for the young man found dead in the cherry grove. He lost his body hair with the rest of them, but his dreadlocks remained intact until his murderer scalped him. I asked the girls, whose dreadlocks were still intact, were they affected in other areas of their bodies and they said no.

I had the boys take me to their dorm rooms; they didn't share a common shower or use the same toiletries. They periodically ate in the cafeteria, but seldom together. The three that were having sex had different sex partners. Their prior trips to the campus medical center revealed nothing to them. They didn't have a clue as to why their hair was gone.

What they did know was that all their gigs left with their hair. They hadn't secured a single booking for the band since the hair loss. The competing all black reggae band was booked most nights and double booked on the weekends. None of the group members said it, but it was clear where their suspicion laid. They told me the police never questioned the other group or anyone else on campus about the boy's death.

That night I went to hear the other band play. What? Yeah I went to a college bar and to be honest with you, that reggae stuff ain't that bad. At least not the way those boys played it. They were a nice group boys, all from Kingston, Jamaica. They actually got here because of reggae music. They were paid a stipend through the university's anthropology department.

No, I don't mean the music department; anthropology is what I said. They were really a nice group of boys. It was a shame they got caught up in all that hateful chaos, but at least they got a record deal out of it. I hear tell they're in London, recording an album.

Oh yeah, you know the university got them out of here in a hurry. You're right. It wasn't really their fault they didn't make themselves the object of a study. Their interest was making music. If it wasn't for them two young black girls, the truth might have never come out. What? Yeah, they left here too. They went to London with the band.

The white boys are still here, but they play heavy lead stuff. What? Metal, lead, whatever; they aren't playing reggae. The university changed their minds for them. That's not true; I don't blame everything on the university, but, if them boys didn't attend the university, they would still have hair; they would still be playing Reggae; and the one that died in the cherry grove would still be alive. What? What do you mean you still don't know how I put it all together. Haven't you been listening? The two young girls was the key.

I hung around the campus for a week or two talking to students and the men that run the physical plant. I thought maybe someone had poisoned the boy's water. I figured if I found out who did that, I would have the murderer. There was nothing up that tree the boy's water couldn't have been tampered with without affecting their whole dormitory.

It turns out I was right about the poison, but I was looking in the wrong direction. I might have stayed stuck on that track if it wasn't for the boy's girlfriend. She insisted I follow around the Jamaican band. I thought it was a silly idea at the time, plus my feet weren't up to traipsing behind them young boys all day. But she was paying the bill, so I followed them.

One of the first things I noticed was the girls from the other band coming around the Jamaican band. At first they were distant, but after a couple a days they were right in the mix with them Jamaican boys, up on stage singing and everything. I let them see me, but they didn't act the least bit ashamed of their new friends. They weren't hiding. It was clear that they wanted to be part of the Jamaican reggae band.

I stopped following them through the days and started catching the shows at night. A fella as old as me knows different ways to skin a cat. Eventually, everyone involved showed up at the clubs.

When the baldheaded boys showed up, I expected trouble, but there was none. They sat down at their table and waved to the girls as if nothing was wrong. Now, that confused me. If those girls were in their band, why weren't the upset about them singing with the Jamaican band?

I had to ask one of them. I wasn't trying to start a fight. I merely wanted to understand and the young baldheaded boy explained it to me as plain as day. "They were artists," he said, "and as artists, they knew that other artists must do their art to be happy."

They understood those girls had to sing the same as they had to play their instruments. He said an artist must create art to be happy. He was happy the girls were creating and doing their thing.

Looking around the club nightly, I began to notice a scholarly looking woman at every show. What? Yes, I went to every show, I was doing my job okay? Ah, forget you! I already told you I liked the music the way them boys played it . . . so what if the place was filled with college kids? The music was good.

There was something vaguely familiar about the scholarly-looking woman, but I couldn't put my finger on it at the time. One thing was certain, she enjoyed the reggae music. She danced on the stage when the girls weren't there. If she wasn't dancing, she was sitting at a table with her head swaying to the beat while she wrote down notes.

However, the moment the two young black girls arrived, she'd get stiff as a board. If she was dancing when they walked in, she immediately stopped and took her seat. She'd sit at her table rigid. Shortly after the girls' arrival she would hurriedly make her exit.

I asked one of the Jamaican boys about her. He couldn't answer me for grinning. Sitting at the bar table, each one whispered my question to the next, causing everyone at the table to smile except me. Finally, the lead singer answered my question with a grin on his face, "benefactor" is what he called her. She was an anthropologist and it was her work that caused them to be at the university.

Confused again the next morning, I called the murdered boy's girlfriend. Being a university student, I thought she could explain the process a little better to me. She all but bit my head off and told me I was barking up the wrong tree. She also said she wasn't paying me to hang out in bars. She slammed the phone down so hard my ears rang for minutes after.

That night at the show the anthropologist returned. I positioned myself not to be seen and put all my attention on her. As before she danced, sat and took brief notes. When the girls took the stage, she stiffened, but she didn't become rigid. She stood and walked over to the table were the girls were sitting.

The waitress blocked her from my view for a second. When I saw her again, she was situated at the girl's table. After their song the girl's joined her. The chatter appeared friendly for a moment or two but the girls' faces suddenly went blank, then the anthropologist stood and left.

I immediately went to their table and inquired about what was discussed. They said she wanted to include them her study. They were delighted initially because they understood the study to include only Jamaican-born reggae singers. Being part of the study meant more gigs. All the local bars had reggae night because the university co-sponsored the night for the study.

Their other band wasn't right for the study because they weren't Jamaican. The anthropologist told them the spirit of the music wasn't the same. The other band interfered with her study, but now, since the girls were singing with the Jamaican group, things would work out fine. She told them when primitives sang together they always brought spirit to music.

What? Yes . . . she said primitives. The next morning I tried like heck to make an appointment with her, but Ms. Anthropologist was out for the day and her machine wasn't accepting calls. Now I know why; she was getting ready for that night's show.

I had it in my mind to report the anthropologist to whatever authority handled racist statements. I planned on starting with the office of the university president and working my way down. When

I went to the girls' dorm room, I found both of them sick. I didn't like it at all. I made them get up and go to the medical center with me.

Somehow they'd come in contact with a poisonous pepper indigenous to Jamaica. The girls said they had only eaten in the cafeteria. My mind immediately went to the anthropologist. She could have put something in their drinks the previous night.

I went out searching for the band members to ask them about the peppers. I found the lead singer. He knew about the pepper and he knew how to fix a sweet drink that would nullify the toxic effects. I told him to take it to the girls. I also insisted that he and the band perform that night. The anthropologist went to extremes to remove the girls. I wanted to see what she had planned.

That night at the show I was sitting in the back of the bar with Old Sheriff. He hadn't believed a word I told him. He went because I reminded him of three hundred and fifteen town votes our church carried and how he'd only won his last election by eighty votes. Oh yeah, that got him up.

When the Jamaican boys got up stage and started singing, who do you think walks in? That's right, she walked her hateful behind right up on stage. She had made a wig out of the dead boys dreadlocks and was singing that reggae just as good as one of the young sisters. You could have parked my Chevy truck in Old Sheriff's mouth.

Well, that's just about the end of it. Oh, I didn't tell you about the girlfriend. I don't tell too many folks this part because it was kind of confidential. Old Sheriff only found out because the girlfriend secured counsel for the anthropologist. Turns out that the anthropologist is the girlfriend's mama. Could you imagine paying to have your own mama tracked down?

Now, the rest of the story comes from the eavesdropping Old Sheriff did while he had the anthropologist in the town lockup. I can't and won't vouch of its accuracy. According to Old Sheriff, the girlfriend's mama told her to stay away from that young white boy with the dreadlocks. I'm pretty sure what I'm about to tell you came from the anthropologist because I have never heard Old Sheriff say nothing fancier than "croissant."

The hateful anthropologist told her daughter that the dead boy and his friends were culture thieves. They were fools who emulated a cultural experience grown from oppression they could never survive if it was upon them. The pepper was to immolate them for cultural order. She believed they didn't recognize the dangers of their cavalier mimicking. They didn't see that their actions threatened the fragile balance of the oppressed and the oppressors. She said she wanted them all dead.

The oppressors cannot shadow the oppressed. The foolish mimes didn't recognize their own cultural superiority to such primitives. No, the minstrels were not good company for her daughter or any other Western woman.

Then, according to Old Sheriff, her daughter asked her "was the original better?" Old Sheriff said the hateful anthropologist broke out laughing and hasn't stopped yet. Last I heard, the county judge was talking about sending her to the state nuthouse. Yes, Siree, that was my first and last case all wrapped up into one.

I am finished with the detective business. One case was enough. Does your mama still want that office couch for her beauty palor? Good, I'll have it delivered tomorrow. Well I'm about ready to go. You are dropping me at the laundromat right? Good. Thanks a lot. Let's get on out of here.

5

Things Done Changed

I stand here, watching his recently revealed gut rise and fall while he sleeps in my three-legged recliner, which he levels with old Jet magazines and TV Guides. The recliner is less than a year old. He broke it, moving it from my place to his. Fixing it requires him to go to the furniture store and buy a new screw-in leg. He'd rather balance it with magazines than take a twenty minute drive—triflin.'

I stand here watching him. There was a time when I enjoyed watching him. Watching his powerful yet graceful movements on the tennis courts mesmerized me. His backhand still causes opponents to cower. There was a time when he was something for me to watch; a time when my eyes willed themselves to him; a time when seeing him pleased me—but no more. That time is gone.

I stand here watching him. The more I see of him, the more revolting things I notice. Three weeks. I have only lived with him for three weeks and I can no longer stand the sight of him. Perhaps if he was half the man he appeared to be when I met him, the disgust I feel toward him wouldn't be as consuming. Standing over him with packed suitcase in hand, I am fighting the desire to swing this bag with all my might into his pudgy stomach.

I stand here watching him. His gut is a prime example of his half maleness. When I met him, I thought his stomach was as flat as mine. Thirty minutes out of each one of my days goes to keeping my stomach firm and flat. I was deceived into believing he dedicated time to achieving his flat stomach. But no, nothing was further from the truth.

His flat stomach was due to the thick elastic band he wore for a back brace. The brace held his disc in place and it also tucked his pudgy stomach away. He told me the brace had to stay on during all physical activity; that included love making, so I never saw him without it until last week. He doesn't wear the brace around the house when he's relaxing.

I stand here watching him. I could have lived with the gut. If it had not been accompanied by other man destroying imps, such as hairy ears. When I found the hair removing lotion in his toiletry bag, it confused me. I knew he shaved with a straight razor because I enjoyed watching him do it and I knew his body hair was limited to his chest, therefore I didn't see the need for the lotion.

When I asked him about it, he showed me the stubble in his ears. He then dipped a cotton swab in the lotion, and removed the hair from his ears. Goose bumps claimed my whole body during his demonstration. He told me if he didn't remove the hair twice a month, it would grow long enough to braid. After that revelation, he dropped dramatically on my sex appeal chart.

I stand here watching him. I am a grown woman, a part time college student with enough hours to have senior standing. I have my own job, my own car and I had my own apartment until I moved in with this . . . this . . . this less than.

I stand here watching him. He is the first man I have lived with and my second lover. However, I do not believe that one has to be engaged in frequent sexual encounters to find a suitable companion. Prior to us moving forward in the sexual area, I was certain we were a compatible couple; at least I thought we were. God, I want to hit him with this suitcase. I have been played by a less than; less than me, less than any man I ever dated and surely less than the man I'd been intimate with before him.

I stand here watching him. No, hitting him isn't enough. I need to cause him some real pain. He undeservingly became privy to my intimacies. A less than . . . knows me well. How did it happen? I know how it happened; I kept watching him at the Jackson Park tennis courts. Dark brothers look good to me in white shorts; and I noticed him at several functions at the DuSable Museum. I bumped into him twice at the

Regal, but it wasn't until I heard him sing at the Gospel Fest did I decide to return his smiles. What a fool I was, I should have kept him ogling.

I stand here watching him. What kind of man sings in a Christian choir and is not a Christian? This sleeping deceiver right here is the kind. Maybe if I dropped my suit case on his neck? That would cause him some pain, make him hoarse for awhile. No, Jesus gave him that gift. He sings with such an anointed baritone voice that Christians, especially, the sisters, get happy from the first line of his solos. Oh, he can call the spirit in the room, his voice is truly anointed, but one blessing from the Lord doesn't make up for all his other short comings, not by far. He is a heathen and a deceiver, and that makes us unevenly yoked. I am justified in leaving him.

I stand here watching him. Everything about him is false, driving that Mercedes like it's his. What did he tell me, it was one of many. Yeah, one of many on his sister's car lot. Phony! He's just a damn phony. His sister provides his car and his brother, the retail buyer, gets him his clothes and he lives rent free. This is his mother's courtway building. No wonder he always cool and at ease, everything he needs is provided for him. The man is blessed and he doesn't even know it. Heathen.

I stand here watching him. He's smiling in his sleep, even in his sleep his smile is slender. He is careful not to show those missing molars and decaying incisors. What could he be dreaming about that has him smiling so?

I stand here watching him. I should wake his wicked butt up. He'll probably let go of one of those long farts, like he does when I wake him up in the mornings. He goes for a full minute and tries to acts like he's not aware of it. He farts rolls over and falls back to sleep: funky devil and just rotten on the inside.

I stand here watching him. He told me he was a couple of years older than me. I'd like to know in what language is fifteen, a couple. I would have never thought he was that old, but his driver's license don't lie. Now, I know why he shaves his head, to keep the gray hairs away.

I stand here watching him. My father told me a righteous man wouldn't ask a good Christian woman to live with him, and a God fearing Christian woman wouldn't consider it under any circumstances. I told my father things were different today. Black Christian woman have to hold a good man, and if it meant living in sin for a short while . . . well . . . God is a forgiving God. Oh, I should have listened to my father.

I stand here watching him. Three weeks ago I would have slapped the Virgin Mary for this man. That was before I knew how many women he had living here before me. Now, I wouldn't give a wet food stamp for him. Maybe I should knee him in his privates. I wonder how did the other eight women that lived here before me leave; did any of them hurt him? He told me I wasn't the first woman to live here with him, but I didn't think I would be the one to complete his baseball roster.

I stand here watching him. I can't help wondering were the other women disgusted? Did they feel deceived? Did they know he was a less than? Did one of them put that scar on his neck? Did one of them cause the cap on his front tooth? Did one of them split his ear lobe? Is one of them responsible for the twitch in his left cheek whenever he sees grits boiling?

I stand here watching him. What should I leave him with? After all, I'm player number nine, I completed the team. My exit should have some sort of closure to it, nothing criminal but defiantly something memorable.

I stand here watching him as his eyes blink open. Hey, baby he says, he was just dreaming about me. He was thinking about how lucky he was to have a woman like me. Not lucky he says, blessed to have a woman like me. He would be a fool not to do everything in his power to keep my love.

I stand here watching him. I can't believe I'm listening to this crap. He's reaching into blue jean pocket and pulls out a little black box. He says he knows he's not a spring chicken, but he's not on his last leg either. He hasn't been a saint he says, but from all his backsliding the one thing he knows is a good woman, and he has a good one in me. He's opening the little black box. Lord, have mercy, it would make Liz Taylor blink.

I stand here watching him. He was going to ask me Sunday after he joined church, but his dream about me made him feel so good he couldn't wait. If I say yes, he's going over to my father's house and formally ask for my hand in marriage—if this is what I want.

I stand here watching him, and things done changed.

6

A Broken Rule

Her heart is beating so fast and making so much noise that she wonders if Robert can hear it. She can't believe how cool it feels to stretch up for a kiss. Renee is actually on her tippy toes in the vestibule, all five feet ten inches of her, is stretching up for the kiss and what a kiss it is, even his lips feel strong. This is where she belongs, wrapped up in his thick arms and hanging off his broad shoulders. She might not have made him wait so long and beg so hard had she'd known he kisses like this.

She hears the key enter the lock, she hears the tumblers fall, she even hears the door open but she doesn't budge from the comfort of Robert's arms. What she's hearing seems far away and not important. What's important is the strong embrace and mind-trancing kiss that she is involved in. Why had she waited so long for this? It isn't until she hears the door slam and her father calling her name does she connect the sounds.

Oh man! She is busted. In a spilt second she is out of Robert's embrace and standing before her father. With her father in the vestibule the spacious white entryway with a checkerboard tiled floor becomes crowded. She is standing between Robert and her father looking down at her scuffed pink gym shoes with her two very long Pocahontas braids hanging. She is wondering what her father will say and how embarrassing will it be in front of Robert.

"Renee, when your company leaves, which will be now! I want to talk to you. Excuse me young man."

It only takes him a step and a half to leave the large area.

That wasn't that bad, she was expecting a lot worst. Her father wasn't in the vestibule five seconds, but it seemed like an hour. She and Robert both blew a deep sigh of relief when he left.

"Man, Renee, I'm sorry. I didn't even hear him."

She turns around to face him again. Of course he didn't hear him. How could he with a kiss like that in progress?

"I didn't hear him either. So it wasn't your fault no need to be sorry."

She leans into him. With her father gone from the vestibule and out of her sight she stretches up for another kiss. Robert stops her.

"Wait a minute girl your dad is home and he said I got to go."

"Scared?" She asks still reaching up to him.

"Yeah! He's bigger and taller than me and he was nice enough not to snap on me. I ain't the one to push a man in his own house. If you want me to go in there with you and talk to him, I will. I don't want to . . . but if you think it will help I'll go."

"That's sweet of you." She hasn't moved an inch from him. She keeps her eyes in his face until he returns her gaze. "But you don't have to do that."

She moves in quickly before he can turn his head. The kiss is a continuation of the first one but when she feels herself slipping into the same far away place she breaks the embrace and quickly opens the front door. No sense in completely pissing her father off.

"You're right you'd better leave before he snaps on both of us."

Renee sees Robert is surprised by the kiss and obviously disorientated by its abrupt end. Robert tells her, "Girl you butt wild." He steps by her and out the door. "Call me at my daddy's shop. I'll be working there until about eight."

He adjusts his book bag on his shoulder and gives her an earnest look, "I really do need your help with this math."

He bends down to her and pecks her on the cheek. Renee responds by licking his neck. She sees his body shiver involuntarily. He steps out of her range. "You need to stop that."

He looks so sexy to her in his baggy faded jeans and with his wavy black hair. His looks more Philippino than African American, but he never talks about being mixed and she likes that about him. She never talks about being bi-racial either; everyone at school accepts her and him for black and she likes it like that. It's easier. Most people have never even heard of the island her mother is from. By the time she spells Oahu and offers the geography lesson on Hawaiian Islands she could have just said she was African American with a light complexion and not have to put up 'grass skirt' type questions. Which she can't answer because she has never seen her mother's island; her mother being an orphan has always told her that the family in their house was all the family she cared about.

"You know you ought to stop frontin' like that! If you're daddy wasn't here, you wouldn't even be given me all this freaky rhythm." Robert said backing completely out of her reach.

"My daddy wasn't here a minute ago and I gave you a little freaky rhythm." She says in a voice not loud enough to carry off the porch or back into the house.

"Yeah, but you knew he was coming. You ain't slick. You frontin' and I know it but call me anyway. See ya!" He takes the stairs down three at a time.

"I ain't frontin'!" She yells at his back with a pseudo attitude.

"Yeah right! You better go on in that house youngster and get your spanking!"

She slams the door on him but behind it she is smiling. She isn't frontin'. He is lucky he made it to first base and he knows it. Shoot it was only his second time coming over.

She stood in the vestibule and thought about running straight upstairs to her room and putting her father off until her mother came home. He is always calmer in front of her mother, less punitive. Her mother was also calmer and less punitive when he was present, but when alone both of them were strict enforcers of the rules.

She broke the 'No company when no one is home rule'. No company meant, especially, no boy company. This was a major offense and with both of them present her chances of receiving the maximum penalty is less.

"Renee! Is your company gone?"

Her father bellows from the kitchen. Hiding in her room is out. She checks herself in the cast iron trimmed mirror that is hung on the vestibule's largest wall. All the buttons on her yellow dress are fastened and in place. She's wearing no lipsticks so she has no smudges. The only thing that's out of the ordinary is the red flush that her risen in her sand colored cheeks. She can't wait until her color returns to normal with her father calling, so she takes a deep breathe and heads for the kitchen.

Her father is bent over with his head buried in the refrigerator. She watches him before she speaks. He is responsible for her height. No matter were he goes his presence in a room is large. He pulls his head from the refrigerator with a plate of broiled chicken and a can of beer. Standing erect he completely blocks the double sided chrome refrigerator from her view, he is a lot bigger than Robert, but not much taller. He sits at the blond oak kitchen table and points his finger to the chair at the opposite end of the table that seats six. He has taken off his suit coat and loosened his tie. To Renee he looks relaxed, maybe he isn't going to trip that bad.

"What's up, Daddy?" she tries to sound as cheerful as possible.

"'Don't 'what's up Daddy me. Bring me the salt from the cabinet before you sit down."

"You mean the 'lite salt' don't you."

"Did I saw 'lite-salt'?"

"No, but Mama said. . ."

"Did I ask you what your mama said? I said bring me the salt." He looks at her sternly.

The smart thing to do would be to hand him the salt and sit quietly down, however she decides to say, "But mama said the doctor said you're not to have it and I'm not supposed to give it to you."

Her father stands abruptly from his chair walks past her to the cabinet, opens it and grabs the salt shaker. He returns to the table and drops his weight in the chair leaving the cabinet open.

"One day you're going to learn to do what I tell you to do when I tell you to do it. I'm getting tired of all this sass." He's not looking at her his attention is on his plate and the salt he is shaking over it.

Renee doesn't respond because she knows there is no correct response. Her father taught never feed into an argument. He often told her 'two hot heads make only sparks'. When she looks in the open cabinet, she doesn't see the sky blue box the 'lite salt' comes in. When she closes the cabinet, she remembered her mother asking her to substitute all the salt in the salt shakers with the 'lite-salt'. Her mother must have gotten tired of waiting for her to do it and did it herself. A knowing smile crosses her face as she sits at the table and watches her father salt his chicken.

"Daddy, I think Mama had something special in mind for that chicken."

"Look, Renee, I've been fifteen years old before. I know what you're trying to do and it's not going to work. You're in trouble, so you can stop all these childish distractions."

He split a chicken wing apart and pulled a bone through his teeth striping the flesh from it. Now his eyes are on her.

Looking down from his eyes she says, "Really, Daddy, Mama was saving that chicken."

"Well that's something I will have to worry about later. If I were you I'd be concerned with an explanation for that young man being here."

She looks up and finds his eyes still on her. She wants to look away, but again his training enters her mind, 'liars dart their eyes'. She looks him evenly in his eyes.

"An explanation?" Renee's face takes a querulous expression. "I need an explanation?"

Of course she needs an explanation and a darn good one. She doesn't think her father would appreciate the truth. She wanted privacy from the neighbors and bypasses as her tongue danced with Robert's; so, she invited him in for a few minutes.

"Yes, Renee, I believe you do need an explanation. No, I know you need one."

She sees no wavering in her fathers eyes, no chance that maybe he will consider a lesser punishment.

His forehead is wrinkled, his jaws are tight and he eyes have narrowed. This is the look that as a little girl meant a bad whipping was certain. As an adolescent it meant a slap on the butt and hours of quiet time, but at fifteen it meant no money and grounded for a month. This is his don't-play-with-me look and it is encased in a stone hard expression. Looking at her father she notices his closely cropped hair could use a trim, he is getting a little fuzzy around the ends. Normally, she would tell him, but this isn't the time.

He is this serious because the rule she broke is a major offense. Major offenses jeopardize the safety of her and the family. He is going to trip hard over this if she can't get him to listen, but that is the problem; she doesn't have anything for him to listen to.

"Daddy, does it have to be this way?"

Asking an off-the-wall but related question is a stalling technique she'd seen her mother use on him. Her parents are constant debaters and in her book her father rose the better points, but he consistently lost to her mother's filibustering techniques. Her mother never stopped talking in a debate, despite how illogical the statements, she kept talking and that usually wore him out.

"What way, Renee?" He reaches down to his plate and separates a chicken leg from its thigh.

"You know, Daddy, you prosecute and I try to defend."

She sees a couple of wrinkles leave his forehead and his brown eyes open a bit. He is listening to her.

"Is that how you see it, Renee, as if I'm prosecuting you?" He takes a bite from the chicken leg. She thinks she sees concern in his eyes. If he has concerns about being fair or doubts his fairness, he will wait and consult with her mother.

"Yeah, I do!"

No sooner than the words left her mouth she knows she has blown her chance. The first mistake is saying yeah to him. 'Yeah is for your friends. You do not use it with me or any other adult': he hates being "yeahed". The second was her tone even she heard the bad attitude in it. She reacted too quickly to his concerned eyes and possible doubt.

She watches his eyes narrowing and more of his words enter her thoughts, 'guilt makes one impatient'.

"I beg your pardon." He opens his thumb and forefinger and lets the bitten chicken leg fall to his plate. It clanks.

Desperate but trying to remain calm she offers, "Excuse me, Daddy . . . what I meant to say was . . . 'Yes, Daddy, I do feel as though you are prosecuting me'."

He opens his beer and looks through her. He doesn't pick the beer up; he leaves it open and on the table.

"Well, Renee, I guess your right. Those are the roles we play."

She thinks she sees a slight smile cross his dark brown face but it was quickly gone. "After all you did break the rules and by doing that you force me into the role of prosecutor and judge and yourself into the role of defendant. These are the roles your actions created. Next time, baby, don't break the rules."

It wasn't a smile she saw, it is a smirk and it is now covering his whole face. She knows that smirk, she knows it well. It is the same smirk she gives people she defeats at a chess competition It is the same smirk she gave the salutatorian in eighth grade that tried to cheat his way to her valedictorian spot. It is that, 'I've not only beat you, but I beat up well' smirk. He picks up his beer and sips it.

"The explanation please."

She has neither lie nor explanation, but with her mother's filibustering technique in her mind she goes for another question.

"Does that seem fair to you, Daddy, that you are both prosecutor and judge?"

She watches him take two long sips out of beer. He fingers the excess beer from the corners of his mouth and belches.

"I'll tell you what, Renee. In this case I'll simply be the judge and because I witnessed the violation, there is no need for a prosecutor and as the judge I say you're guilty."

She hears the seriousness in his tone and she sees the completion in his expression. He's tired of talking.

"Now. What was that boy doing in here?"

He wants an answer and it isn't fair because she has none for him, not one that will stop the punishment. It isn't fair.

"This isn't right, Daddy, it's just not right. It's not fair!"

Her father drains the beer and crumbles the can with one hand.

"Okay. Lets try this another way. What was the boy doing in here when no one was home?"

"I'm a member of this family, Daddy, I was home."

"What was the boy doing here when no adult was home and trust me child if you give me another smart mouth answer you will regret it. Now is that right and fair enough for you?"

He is talking to her as if she is ten years old and this offends her. Not only is he being unfair he is being insulting as well.

"No, it's not fair . . . the whole thing isn't fair!"

"What whole thing?"

"You!"

"What?"

"You are not being fair. Your rules are not fair. I am fifteen years old. Old enough to decide who is and who is not a threat to me and this family. The rule is not fair! And your question is not fair."

"Are you going to tell me what that boy was doing here?"

"That's my business, Daddy."

"What did you say?"

"I said I am not telling why Robert was here because that is my business. Being fifteen years old I am entitled to have personal busi. . . "

Renee didn't see her father move, but suddenly the whole kitchen table flips over, his plate and chicken scatters. She jumps back and loses her footing. She reaches for the sink, but slips hitting her forehead on the counter that edges the sink. She sees stars as she falls to the floor.

She attempts to blink her vision clear. Her father is standing over her. She reaches for him, but he doesn't help her up instead he yells, "This is my house! And as long as you are living in it you follow my rules! Fifteen or fifty, my house, my rules!" He pounds his fist on the sinks edge above. Did he see her fall and hit her head she wonders?

"You understand me, Renee?"

She is looking at him. She sees his finger pointing at her, but she can no longer make sense of his words. She hurt herself and he is still fussing at her? Her tears add blurriness to her sight, her breath shortens and she can't catch it. She has to gasp for air.

"Do you understand me Renee?"

She looks up from the floor, she wants to tell him she doesn't understand but all she can verbalize is gasps for air. No matter how deep of a breath she takes it's not enough air. She tries to stand, but she collapses to the floor. From the floor next to the toppled kitchen table she finds that she cannot catch a breath. Her chest is getting tight. She folds in pain. Her father moves the table aside to get to her. Unable to breath she didn't try to answer his question. He scoops her up from the floor and cradles her in his arms.

"Baby, are you okay? I'm sorry, baby. Breathe baby! Breathe!"

As if by his command air fills her lungs and she is able to breathe, she sobs against his chest.

Upstairs in her room he stretches her out on her bed and leaves her to her weeping. Not since she was a small child had she cried so. What was it that had brought on such tears as a child? Oh yeah, it was the whipping she got when she was seven years old. She'd thought it was a good idea for her father's aquarium fish to swim around in the toilette. They looked bored with the tank and she truly thought the exotic fish would appreciate a change of scenery. And she thought it would really be fun for them if she flushed them down the toilet. It was like a ride at Six Flags because they would certainly swim back up through the water after she flushed them down. She waited, but they didn't swim back up.

When her father asked her what happened to his fish she told him he she didn't know and he believed her until her mother started questioning her and she got all mixed up and told half the truth. When her father heard her say she flushed them down the toilet, he grabbed her and started spanking her that second.

Later after she told him she thought they would swim back up, he said he was sorry for spanking her and soon after that they went to Disney World for the first time. She had an explanation for her actions then, today she had no explanation—except that Robert was tall, fine and kissed real good. She puts her hand on her forehead and feels a lump developing.

"A hickey! I'm going to have a knot on my head." She wants to raise up and go to the mirror, but the energy isn't there. The hickey will be on her forehead, but the back of her head is where she feels the most pain. Her father said he was sorry and she believed him, he wouldn't hurt her deliberately but she knew she'd played a part in it too.

She broke the rule and tried to cover it up. She was wrong. She should have just told him Robert came in to use the bathroom or something and took the punishment for having company. Maybe she would apologize to her father. No, not yet, she would wait and see what her mother's input will be. If it is left to her daddy, she is sure she would be on her way to Disney World. A smile inches across face as she slips into a dream of Mickey and Goofy dancing around her and Robert.

7

Life on T. V.

The bus is ragged and the ride is rugged. Timothy sits in the last row of seats at the rear of the city bus. He is wide-awake, but he wishes he were drowsy. If he fell asleep, the ride wouldn't be so miserable. The smell of urine and spilled wine offends his nose. The hard plastic and rubber seats of the bus assault his butt and back with each pothole. Last night he rode down the same street in Tweet's Caddy and none of the potholes were felt. His grandmother told him doing the right thing is always easier than doing the wrong thing. He found that not to be true. It is much harder to get up every morning and go to school than it is to hang out with Tweet and The Family. The hardest part of school is getting there.

Every morning he tossed around the idea of playing sick to remain in the comfort of the big bed his grandmother brought him. The king sized bed was one of the few places where he didn't feel cramped. The idea of playing sick quickly leaves his mind when he thinks of his grandmother's sick remedy; she gives cod liver oil for everything from a cold to an earache.

Once free of the bed's comfort the smell of breakfast motivates him forward, neither he nor his grandmother is supposed to eat the food she cooks for breakfast. At 315 pounds the school nurse begged him to diet. He ignored her just as he ignored the countless county hospital doctors. He was from a big family, his mama is big and grandmother is big. True he's the biggest, but he is a man. He is supposed to be bigger besides the football coach isn't complaining about six-foot two-inch frame.

His nose told him what to expect for breakfast, the aroma of buttered biscuits was detected from buttered toast the scent of bread was stronger with the biscuits. The aroma from Mississippi red sausages cut straight through his sinuses the spices smoked more in the skillet than the sage in the in sausage patties. With fried eggs it was the crispy edges of the whites he smelled compared to the broken yokes of scrambled eggs. A smile snuck across his face despite the miserable bus ride his grandmother knew how to get him out of the bed.

With football season being over the only things he looked forward to at school is selling his product and seeing his boys. He did enough schoolwork to pass and that was it. If it wasn't for his grandmother's urging, he wouldn't have done the amount of work he did. He never felt comfortable in school. The chairs are too small and he saw no real purpose in going. School didn't teach him how to get rank in The Family. It didn't teach him how to weigh quarter ounces of weed or rock up cocaine. It didn't teach him how to get a dope selling spot and run it twenty-four hours a day. School didn't teach him how to get rich, not the way he'd seen people get rich.

The teachers at school talked about a life that wasn't his—a make-believe fairy tale life. It was the same with the school nurse that told him to diet. In her world thin men are cool in his world big men are cool. Few people tried to take from a big man. When he walks through his world, the greetings of 'Hey Big Man' makes him feel at ease. He is a big man.

He is certain being big earned him his football status. Not only was he the only freshman on the varsity team, he is the only player that starts in two positions—nose tackle and center. As a nose tackle he led the team in recovered fumbles and touchdown conversions. He is a football star, but he doesn't see it leading to any money. Plenty of former high school football stars live in his world flat broke.

The coach told him would have scouts looking at him next year. He didn't believe the coach. The coach was trying to get him to play harder. Tweet told him, "White people are always trying to play with a Black man's mind. They get him thinking they want to help him; when all along they're helping themselves."

Nope, he didn't believe the coach. He played football because he liked it, not to get to the pros. It's like Tweet says, if he keeps his head on straight and remained focused on what is real, he will be rich when he finishes high school. Real life is what he sees everyday, people spending money on drugs. Tweet was twelve when he started getting his own work from The Family. He now runs three twenty-four hour dope spots and isn't old enough to buy beer.

The brakes on the bus squealed as it came to a stop in the intersection. The police have the intersection blocked. Through the window Timothy is able to see four squad cars surrounding a red pick up truck. It's Micky's truck. Three of the police have Micky and one of his boy's spread across the hood of one of the squad cars frisking them while the others are searching through the truck.

Micky isn't dumb enough to ride with work in a tricked out truck. Timothy sat back and waited for the police to finish. Minutes later the bus pulled off, and, so did Mickey and his boy. Timothy caught his eye and his grin as he and his boy drove off. Yeah, the boys in The Family keep their business tight they hardly ever got busted.

By the time the bus made it to school Timothy decided it isn't a good day for school. When he steps of the bus, he heads straight for the pay phone to page Tweet. The Family uses pagers and public phones instead of cell phones. Timothy didn't understand why but that is the way it is, pay phones and pagers no cell phones. He'd spend the day hanging with Tweet and playing Madden if he came and got him. Tweet didn't like to help him ditch school, but he hadn't ditched in months. He figured it would be cool with Tweet. While pushing in Tweet's numbers a heavy hand shakes his shoulder. He turns away from the pay phone and sees the coach. He hangs up the phone.

"What's up, Coach?"

"I've been looking for you, Tim. I got somebody I want you to meet. Follow me to my office."

"Coach I got first period class."

Timothy is trying not to go into the school. He can't beep anyone from the pay phones in the school and once he is inside it's a little hard to get back out.

"Don't worry about it. I'll clear it with the teacher. What you got Spanish first period?"

"Yeah." Timothy is a little surprised the Coach knows his schedule and it is obvious he was going to have to go with him. Maybe he could sneak out at lunch.

When they walked into the Coach's office, Timothy saw the back of a huge man. The man is facing the Coach's T.V. and watching a tape of Timothy's season. Timothy has never seen the tape. The Coach told him he was going to put one together from the team's season, but Timothy thought he was only talking. Watching himself on television made him feel light headed. The Coach put Timothy's best plays on the tape. Man he looked kind of good. He couldn't stop the smile from stretching across his face as he watches himself tearing through offensive linemen. He crushed them. He yelled out loud as he watched himself score the conversion touchdown that won the homecoming game.

"I told you." The Coach says to the huge back. "The kids got focus. It's hard to believe he's only a fourteen."

When the huge back turned around, Timothy knows immediately who he is. He had led the city's team to a Super Bowl victory in the nineties and now he coached a college team.

The huge back thought, "He can focus on the field but how about off the field. I've seen hundreds of kids in this city that had the ability to be Heisman trophy winners, but off the field they didn't care about the game. They didn't know they had a gift."

"What about you young man," the huge man puts his eyes on Tim. "Is football simply something you do or do you want it to make your life better?

"Don't answer me today. I want you to be sure when you answer. I'm going to be in town for a couple days. I'll stop by later in the week for your answer. If you want football to make your life better,

I got a high school outside of this city I'd like to see you go to. Matter of fact it's out of this state.

"Your coach knew when he showed me the tape what I would offer you, so don't feel like you're turning your back on him. He knows what I know. He's seen what I've seen. Too few of you young Black athletes make it when you stay in the city. You got some thinking to do. I want to know how you feel before I talk to your parents.

"You got skill Timothy with the proper training and guidance you could make to the pros. I've never seen a fourteen year old play with your intensity."

Tim sits eating a dry hamburger in the cafeteria at lunch. He couldn't get his mind off of what the huge man asked him, 'Did he want football to make his life better'. He did look good on the T.V. The huge man said he would have to go to school outside of the city, but he couldn't run his business from that far away. And it's just getting to the point were he would soon get his own dope spot. He moved up in Tweet's number picture last month after the number one dope spot came open. He is on the verge of making some serious money.

A couple of his boys are sitting at the lunch table with him, but their conversation doesn't penetrate his thoughts. Did he want football to make his life better? Did he? He didn't think of football in that way. The Family is to make his life. Football is fun nothing serious. The only brothers that made money in that game played on television the pros.

"Man. This is what Tweet is talking about staying focused." He couldn't let outside stuff get into his head. Football is outside stuff.

Tweet and the other Family members made money in his world, the real world. He has to stay focused if he wants to get rich; if he wants to get a tricked out truck; if he wants to wear the best clothes; and if he wants real rank in the Family. By the end of the dry hamburger his mind is made up football is fun. Getting rank in the Family is real. But, man, he did look good on T.V.

He is boarding the bus heading home when he feels his pager vibrating. He checks it and sees Tweets number. He backs off the bus and jogs to the phone.

"Hey, Big Man."

"What's up, Tweet?"

"Got some work for you. You out goods, right?"

"Yeap, finished up at lunch."

"Good, you got about three fifty?"

"You better check your math, brother I got four twenty five for you."

"Cool. You still at school?"

"Yeap."

"Awright, stay put I'll scoop you in about five."

Timothy hangs up the phone, turns away from the booth and finds himself face to face with Coach. He wonders how much of the conversation he had heard. He doesn't have to wonder long.

"If you were talking to the Tweet, I know you best be careful. He's a young man heading for old trouble. And the sad part is his life didn't have to be the way it is. Did you know he was all city wide receiver his junior year?"

"I don't know a Tweet, Coach. You must have heard me wrong."

"Yeah, I'm sure I did. Why don't I stand here with you and see if a white Caddy picks you up. The same one that picked you up twice last week."

"Coach it's a lot of white Caddies in this city."

"You right about that, thousands, but there's only one former NFL coach looking at your tape. You get my meaning? Tim, you stand out like a sore thumb on the football field and on the schoolyard. It's not hard to see what you're doing. You're the biggest young man in the crowd and I'm not the only one that has you on tape Timothy. You hear me Tim?

"Campus security brought me a tape last week. You are a smart young man, you know what I'm saying. They warn everybody once. Consider yourself warned, Timothy. When the Tweet you don't know shows up, ask him about his football days and watch his eyes. Watch his eyes close. I'll talk to you tomorrow if you make it back and I hope you do."

Timothy doesn't watch Coach walk away. He turns and faces oncoming traffic. If campus security had him on tape, maybe he wouldn't be coming back. He could make more money at the neighborhood high school anyway. He only went to this school because his grandmother said it would teach him a trade. Later for Coach and the school, he got a trade. Besides he could walk to the neighborhood school and not have to bother with the bus. When Tweets Caddy pulled to the curb, he slides in without looking back at the school.

After greeting Tweet in The Family way and giving him his money, Timothy sat quietly thinking up away to bring up Tweet's football history and the Coach's warning about campus security. He knew what Tweet would say about the warning; 'Fuck him, transfer schools stay focused'. What he didn't know was what Coach meant about looking into Tweet's eyes.

Coach taught his players to look into the opposing teams eyes on the line. He said a smart player could see fear. He didn't have to teach Timothy to spot fear. Spotting fear in another person's eyes is part of his world and so is hiding his own.

Eyes revealed a lot to Timothy he could tell when his grandmother was really happy because her eyes sparkled. When she was really angry, they thinned and pierced his heart. When she was sad or disappointed they were dull and wet.

When Tweet pulled him up in rank in The Family, he saw jealously and envy in some of his boy's eyes. Despite their congratulatory words their eyes showed the truth. Windows to the soul his grandmother called them. What did the coach want him to see in Tweet's eyes?

"Tweet, Coach was talking about wide receivers today. He said you was one of the best that ever played the. What's up with that?"

He'd wait to tell him about the warning; he wanted to see what Coach expected him to see in Tweet's eyes.

"What do mean what's up with that? He ain't lying. I was one of the best if not the best. All City in my junior year! A couple of scouts was all over me. I played the game like it's supposed to be played, balls to the wall."

Timothy sees the glowing pride in Tweets eyes. Tweet sits erect behind the wheel of the white Caddy as he speaks.

"Coach knows what he talkin' about. What else did he say about me?"

Timothy goaded him on.

"He said you had the hands, the speed and the heart."

"Fo sho! I was faster than every dude on the team. I lettered in track too. Man old coach talkin' 'bout me huh? Ain't that somethin'."

"Yeah, he said you could have had it all."

"Hey! I got it all and I got all without bustin' by back. He tried to sell me that college and NFL dream. Man, I wasn't tryin' to hear that. All the scouts was talkin' about was payin'' fo' college if I played football. Wasn't none of them talkin' 'bout payin' me while I played. I thought about goin' to Canada, but I didn't. I couldn't stand gettin' hit anyway. I took the hits, but, man, it's more to life than gettin' your guts mixed up by a bunch of big cats. I played the game and I played it well. I was smart enough not to get caught up in that dream of makin' the pros. I ain't got time for dreams. I needs to count money not wishes.

"Coach got pissed because I didn't go out for the team in my senior year. Man that was his dream not mine. I know what I am. I know where I belong. I chose the game that chose me. Just like you, Big Man. I was focused on what was real. What the coach tryin' to sell you that dream already?"

"Yeah, he had an old NFL coach talk to me today."

"About what?"

"They were talking about me transferring to some high school out of the state."

"Wow, and you only a freshman! What did you tell him?"

"Nothing."

"What! Why not?"

"I ain't trying to hear that stuff about leaving the city."

"Man don't be a stupid fo."

Targeted bullets that are shattering the driver's window of the Caddy stop Tweet's sentence. The Caddy runs into the side of a brick garage.

Timothy and four other Family members are standing around Tweet in the emergency room ignoring the doctors and nurses request for them to leave. Tweet is in the bed with his whole head bandaged. The doctor cut holes in the bandage to force tubes up Tweets nose and down his throat. Blood soaks through the white bandages were his eyes should be. Timothy feels his knees weakening. He can't look at Tweet's bandaged head, nor can he leave. His own head is beginning to hurt. He tries to put his attention on Tweet's heart monitor, but his vision blurs. He blinks his eyes clear. He watches Tweet's pulse rise over the graph lines on the monitor screen. Some pulses went higher on the graph than others. More yards Timothy thought. Come on, Tweet, keep getting them first downs baby. Timothy silently cheers Tweet on. Each pulse that rose beyond the third line is a first down every fourth pulse that reaches the third line was a touch down. Timothy's vision blurs again. He rubs his eyes.

When he pulls his hands from his eyes, some of Coach's plays are on the monitor screen. Timothy sees Tweet run a fly pattern for a first down. He sees himself run a draw play for a first down. He wiped at his eyes but the images remained on the monitor. Every fourth pulse he or Tweet score a touchdown. Timothy began sweating as he watches himself and Tweet earn first downs and score touchdowns.

On the monitor he sees himself, Tweet, Donovan McNaab, Walter Payton, Terrell Owens and the Fridge. They are all in a huddle waiting for a play. It is Monday Night Football and the coach is on the sideline signaling in plays. The play is to Tweet the long ball. Timothy is on the line next to Fridge the defensive line is white bandage heads with blood soaked eyes. Timothy hiked the ball to McNaab on the second count. He and Fridge held four bloody bandaged head linesman at bay and McNaab puts into flight a perfect spiral. Tweet is stretched to the sky inches away from the ball when the screen flat lined.

Timothy wakes to the sound of a television. He is alone in a hospital room. The bed across from him is empty. He is hooked to an I.V. and his arms are strapped down. He feels unusually relaxed. He knows Tweet is dead. He is sad, but he can't raise any anger.

A news sport show is playing on the television they are recapping the NFL's season. Timothy noticed none of the players got shot in the head. Life on T.V. looks good. He thinks about his tape. Could football make his life better? He decides to listen more to what the coach with the big back has to say. It won't kill him to listen.

8

Our Dance

It was Wednesday night; hump night in my studying routine. I was carrying six classes that quarter and three of them quizzed on Fridays. I was dog-tired and wasn't in the mood for the nightly bull sessions the fraternity house offered. I was headed straight up the stairs to my room when Scott beckoned me to the living room.

At that time I considered Scott a friend. It was his urging and my own desire to make connections for the future that caused me to pledge the predominately white fraternity. As a Black student I knew my grades had to be the top ten percent if I expected to earn an internship at a top corporation. My daddy or none of his friends sat on any corporate boards although the church board he did sit on was instrumental in getting me in school. It was up to me to stay in school and make the right connections that would lead to the right job; thus, my pledging the white fraternity.

That evening I joined five other fraternity brothers that were lounging with Scott in the living room. The topic of conversation was dates for Friday night's dance. Timothy, one of the fraternity brothers who were scheduled to graduate last spring had finally earned enough hours to officially get his degree. He along with ten other students in the same situation rented the faculty banquet hall for the dance. I thought it all absurd, why celebrate failing to finish on time.

Timothy was a chronic slacker who spent his study time guzzling beer and watching pornography tapes. His grades were far below average and he seemed totally unconcerned about them. His cavalier attitude concerning his studies, along with his perverted taste in film, made him one of my least favorite fraternity brothers. His date it appeared for Friday night's dance was a paid escort. This didn't surprise me; I doubted his ability to interact with an educated woman he did not pay.

He sat passing the escort's photograph around and she was voluptuous to say the least. If breast size has anything to do with providing maternal nutrients, this woman could have easily fed every hungry child in Poland and Ethiopia. Her rates were printed on back of the photograph. What she charged for one night was half of what the church sent me for a full quarter's allowance. I simply smiled. I was past being shocked over the dollars my fraternity brothers spent on frivolous whims.

Of the countless dances we've attended as a group, and those we've hosted, never have any fraternity brothers asked me who would be my date. I sat there listening to their list of possible conquest for Friday night and I was becoming quite bored, when Scott mentioned a different name. One never spoken of in the context they were speaking. Certainly they spoke of her when they conversed about academic achievers and when they required tutorial help but they never spoke of her in carnal tones. Scott sat back on the couch rubbing his crotch and spoke as if his conquest was certain. He cut his eyes over to me, trying to gage my reaction to his statement I suppose. My thoughts were masked behind my smile. This was why he delayed me. I sat a few moments before leaving not wanting to reveal my true emotion.

Once in my room I sat on the corner of my bed and smiled. The plan materialized in thought before I hit the top step. I was certain it would end the friendship between Scott and me but my intervention was a must. Perhaps, if he would of spoken of her with some remnants of respect, I would have felt differently. His tone was guttural. He referred to her as brown sugar.

I laid on my pillow prepared for sleep and thought of Brenda's beauty; her classic high cheekbones, full lips, raised forehead and a proud African nose. No, she was not to be polluted by the likes of

Scott. I, who appreciated her poise, never approached her. Not for lack of desire, alas, absence of confidence was the culprit.

Restful sleep was not to be had, doubt and insecurity tossed me all night. The smile that graced my face with the conception of the plan was replaced the next morning with a grimace of dismissal. Across the room a young red head was entangled in Scott's arms asleep. He winked on of his pale green eyes in my direction and put his index finger to his lips and nodded toward our bedroom door.

This was standard operating procedure when Scott's female endeavors slept over. I was to creep out the room without waking the girl. How he convinced them to engage in sexual intercourse with me sleeping across the room was beyond my understanding. With my clothes in tow I left Scott with his most recent conquest.

Waking to the red head in Scot's arms reminded me of his sexual prowess. He slept with a different woman almost every week of the quarter. I had slept with none. Obviously, he knew what to say and when to say it. Were Black women prone to submission from the same words? Would his Don Juan verbiage corral Brenda into his bed? He spoke on the couch as if it was a certainty. I'd woke to no Black women in his arms as of yet, but then again he never spoke of Black women carnally.

Entering my first class of the day, Statistics, and seeing Scott positioning himself behind Brenda in a lecture hall seat, I wished for a lesser adversary, one not six foot two inches tall, one who didn't drive a roadster and one who stuttered over his words in the presence of pretty females, as I did. The only woman who told me I wasn't a bad looking man was my mother, and she didn't say I was attractive, merely, not bad looking. I had all but given up my plan of chivalrous damsel-saving when Scott slung the gauntlet to the floor. Sitting behind Brenda he mimicked fellatio and pointed to my proud looking Black sister. Our fates were sealed; we were engaged in battle.

I have never been ashamed of or embarrassed by my parents professions. My father is an auto body man and my mother works in a preschool. Neither of their incomes led me to carefree abandonment of dollars. I did not own a car. My wardrobe consisted of three pair of jeans, six plain white button down oxfords, a pair of canvas gym shoes and a pair of work boots. For church and dress I owned one brown suit and a pair of black wing tip shoes.

Brenda on the other hand was never seen in the same blouse. When a school quarter ends, a limousine waits at the steps of her sorority house to tote her and several trunks to the airport. The students she dated were all B.M.O.C.'s (Big Men On Campus). They were fraternity presidents, athletic heroes and drivers of fine automobiles. Being greatly aware of our differences in social status was yet another reason for my hesitance in approaching her.

Willing my legs forward I walked down the steps of the lecture hall to the aisle she was sitting. I breathed in deeply and made my way to her seat. Sitting beside her I mentally produced a list of our commonalities. We shared an African American heritage; we were both computer science majors; we were both in our third year of school; we were both in the top ten percent of our class; and she used a yellow hi-liter.

I prayed for a steady tongue throughout most of the lecture, ignoring Scot's kicks to the back of my chair. When the lecture ended, I grabbed her books from under her chair. I stood with them in my arms and asked if I could walk her to lab. Her positive reply and warm smile almost made me lose my footing. When I looked back for Scott, he was gone.

I often enjoyed lab, but never with the intensity of that day. Brenda appeared determined in me knowing that she was quite capable in the lab. Having observed her intelligence for three years, I was not surprised. We worked well together. We thought along similar lines and her logic intrigued me.

After two hours of stammer free conversation my confidence rose a bit. I asked her to lunch she told me no. She was meeting a friend, one of my fraternity brothers, Scott. I asked her did she know him well. She said no, she'd begun tutoring him in Basic only that quarter. Books in arm she left me sitting at the lab table.

Divulging Scott's motive at that point would have been foolish. I needed more information about Brenda. True, I'd never seen her dating a white student, but that didn't necessarily imply that she was opposed to interracial dating. And was interracial dating the problem? How could that be a problem for me the only Black member of a predominately white fraternity? No, the problem was Scott and his intentions.

Would I have been upset if a Black student had matching intentions? What if she liked Scott? Wouldn't I come off like I was a Black militant on a tirade? I asked myself if a Black student planned on compromising Brenda's virtues, would I have gone into action?

I knew what most of the Black students called me behind my back. I was not a loved man on campus, but I didn't attend school to be loved. I attended to improve my position in life, and so did they. If their Black conscious was so high, why didn't they attend a historically Black college? They were playing the identical game as I. They just weren't as committed as I was to making contacts. They attended a mainstream school to earn mainstream money, the same as myself. If I was an Uncle Tom so were they.

Yes, I told myself if I had heard a Black student planning what Scott was planning and with the same disrespectful overtones I would intervene. If Brenda was attracted to Scott, exposing his plan in lab wouldn't have benefit me. I would have appeared either jealous or a racist in her eyes. My original plan was best. I had to gain favor in her eyes. I grabbed my books and ran from the lab to catch her.

Upon entering the cafeteria I approached her and explained that since our next class was together it was only logical that I join her and one of my best friends for lunch. Her face was puzzled, but she smiled and agreed. When Scott entered the cafeteria and saw us eating together, he smiled half heartedly at me and left. I was overjoyed. I was winning.

During the lunch several of her sorority sisters stopped by said hello to her and hesitantly introduced themselves to me. I saw each of them give a look that asked her if their assistance was required in ridding her of my presence. She ignored each look and continued her conversation with me. When we finished lunch, I gathered her books and carried them to class for her.

Approaching the end of our Business Morality class I realized this was the last class Brenda and I had scheduled together until Monday. My panic rose as minutes ticked off the clock. It was a simple question; I counted the words, eight in total. Will you go to the dance with me? Yes or no was all she could say. The problem was what might accompany her no, laughter, utter disgust, pity, snobbery or worst, the dreaded offer of platonic friendship.

I was perspiring and I was certain my tongue was no longer steady with the confidence from lab and lunch. Brenda heard my increased breaths and asked if I was okay. I nodded my head to affirm my physical health, but mentally, I was wrecked. She pulled a monogrammed handkerchief from her small purse and handed it to me. She touched her forehead, indicating that my perspiration was showing. I tried to tell her I didn't want to stain her handkerchief, but my tongue failed me. I sat there holding the handkerchief in my lap with head hung.

She took the handkerchief from me and wiped the perspiration from my forehead. She knew I was gathering my thoughts and she was patient enough for me to bring them to words. All I wanted to do was protect this Black woman from a man with less than honorable intentions. Being honest with myself, I knew my feelings went beyond protecting her.

There were too many obstacles in the way is what I told myself. We couldn't date and really get to know each other. How long could she or would she ignore the looks of her sorority sisters? My plan was to stop Scott from going out with her and sullying her reputation, not to get romantically involved with her.

She was from another world I told myself. Maybe later in life I would be part of it. It would only be the dance, wanting anything more would be foolish. I had to stick to the original plan. Forcing myself to keep in mind that I was protecting her and it was only for one night my confidence returned. Once class ended, I held her hand and asked her to give me a minute.

There was no puzzled look on her face when I asked her to the dance. Her smile was full and her eyes sparkled when she told me yes. If there was a bigger man on campus that afternoon, he was unknown to me. I was without a doubt, The Big Man On Campus.

That night in my room I prepared for the argument Scott and I would have. I would tell him I cared seriously for Brenda and found his statements about her disturbing. I would also warn him never to speak of her that way again. I was looking forward to setting him straight; however, Scott slept elsewhere that night.

My mind was purely evil, the entire night I envisioned Scott in Brenda's room. When I could no longer stand the obsessed, jealous thought, I got up and walked to Brenda's sorority house looking for Scott's car. It wasn't there. It was parked down the street in front of another sorority house. I cursed myself for the insecurity and doubt and went home.

Doubt didn't enter my mind as I buffed my only pair of dress shoes, nor did it enter my mind when I brushed down my brown suit. It didn't show its ugly head as Brenda and I danced the night away. It appeared after the dance when I witnessed Scott walk Brenda outside. Doubt fussed my feet to the floor. Doubt told me of course she preferred him, I was nothing compared to him.

It was Timothy's big-busted escort who freed my feet. She asked me where my girlfriend was. She told me it had been years since she saw two young people so in love. My feet moved by themselves.

When I approached them outside, I heard Scott telling Brenda that she was right about me. I did require a challenge to get into action he said. He told Brenda he hoped that he would find a woman who could read him as well as she read me and cared about him as much as she seemed to care about me. He told her he still didn't see what she saw in me, but, if I was the man she wanted he was happy for her.

Scott said I was funny looking, Brenda told him, no, that I had distinct features. He asked her if he should tell me that they were friends from high school. Brenda answered no, saying that I might feel manipulated. Scott told her she had manipulated me by asking him to act as if he was interested in her. Brenda said, no, she merely gave me the chance to be the Black man of her dreams.

I never told Brenda I heard her and Scott talking that night. However, remembering the event has given me an idea for the inscription in her anniversary gift; our thirtieth, 'From the Black man of your Dreams, Love Thaddeus.' She'll love it.

9

Paid Fo'

It was quiet, but neither one was sleep. For six years they had shared this space. And tomorrow Randolph would be gone. Calvin guessed he was laying in the top bunk grinning from ear to ear. Calvin wanted to be genuinely happy for Randolph, but his own desire for freedom stopped the happiness. He couldn't help wishing that he was the one being released.

Randolph wasn't grinning; he wasn't even smiling. Thirty years was the time he had served. Tears come from his eyes as thoughts he had locked away decades ago claimed his attention.

He thought of his wife, Tamara, a full woman who accepted all his desire. She gave him a small tender son. Raymond was his son's name. The space they took in his conscious mind hurt him deeply. He knew this pain and he knew it could drive men crazy—the pain of wanting. The pain of wanting to feel, to touch and care for what one could not, feel, touch or care for.

The scent of the rose water his wife washed his son's with hair misted from his mind to his nose. He was such a small baby; too small to grow up without a father; and his wife, too much of a woman not to have a man.

Randolph tried to force the thirty-eight-year-old memories to maturity. He tried to picture his son grown and his wife older, but they remained as they were thirty years ago. His son remained a small baby that needed his father's protection and his wife remained a gown woman that needed her husband's desire. He wanted to give them what they needed. He wanted to be the father and husband the memories needed, but even in his mind's eye he was an inmate, and unable touch them.

His wife, a strong smart woman, did what Randolph considered to be the right thing; twenty-seven years ago she divorced him and moved away. He was glad she did it. He couldn't afford to care about people outside the walls of his daily existence. He had seen that type of caring drive men crazy; caring about what they couldn't touch. That wasn't for him thirty years ago and he wasn't going to allow it to be for him now. Thirty years ago he put his wife and new son in his grandpappy's small iron box and he expected them to stay there.

After his grandpappy died, no one in his family could find the key to the old iron box. His father and uncles tried to bust the lock open with a sledge hammer, they tried to cut it with tin snips and they tried to pry it open with a crowbar, but it wouldn't give. Frustrated with the box and satisfied with the papers the bank sent over, they discarded the box in the "heap pile" in back of the barn.

Randolph got the iron box out the "heap pile" and kept it for years. He was never able to open it, but he was able to slide things through the seams. These were things that he never wanted to see again: like his sixth grade report card, the pictures he took at the dime store photo booth and, after the Judge sentenced him; he placed his wife and son inside his grandpappy's box.

Tonight his wife and son escaped the box and brought with them pain of wanting. He rolled over in the bunk and wiped the tears from his shank scarred face.

Calvin heard Randolph tossing around in the bunk above him and figured he was probably dancing a jig to himself, the happy bastard.

"Hey, Randy! You woke, man?"

Randolph didn't hesitate to answer, talking might stop the pain.

"Yeah, Cal. I'm wide awake man."

"Thinking about tomorrow huh?"

"No, not really, young brother, I'm stuck in the past."

"Why you in the past when you about to free? You need to be thinking about the future. Man, if it was me getting out of here, my mind would be on next week's bitches. I told you befo', when I get outta here I'm fucking for a month straight, a different bitch every night."

"Not calling women bitches you ain't."

"Man, I keep telling you, hoes like being called bitches, at least the hoes I want do. So, tell me, Randy, what's the first thing you gonna do when you hit Chi Town and don't tell me you don't know again. You gettin' out tomorrow, nigga, so I know you done figured it out by now. All of Chicago is waiting for you Randy, so what cha gonna do? Tell me man?"

Randolph knew what he was going to do. Six months ago he was informed of the Judge's practice of meeting the men he sentenced at the dispatch gate after they were released. That information helped put his ten-year obsession into a plan.

Initially, Randolph didn't believe it. No man could be that arrogant, to walk up to a man that he had taken years from and extend him a hand to shake. In Randolph's opinion only a man seeking death would do such a thing. Randolph knew what he was going to do upon release, but it was not to be shared with his young cellmate.

"Well, young brother, I'm thinking along the lines of a steak dinner. You made that sound kind of good last week when you was talking about your release plans."

"You ain't jiving a brother is ya, Randy? Man, I would love to lay here tomorrow and think about you eating a steak dinner. You gonna do that fo' real man?"

"I got my partial soaking now."

Randolph saw no harm in giving Calvin a nice thought. He'd find out soon enough what he actually did. Randolph had done it once and seen it done six times. He figured he knew enough about it to pull it off.

He didn't know if the Judge had bodyguards or if the prison guards would have him in their gun sites. The only certainty he had was the fact the Judge would shake his hand and that was all he needed. Once the Judge put his hand in Randolph's it would be over.

Over the years he watched twenty-one men get killed. By far, the worst way to bring death was strangulation. Each time a person was strangled Randolph saw them grasping for their life until the end, wanting not to die. The threat of death brought the strongest wanting. Randolph believed the Judge would benefit from such wanting.

"Get the T-bone steak, man, and don't forget the 'A-1' sauce. When you bite into that sucker, I going to be right there with you man! I swear I'ma know when you swallow that first bite. You hear me Randy? I'ma be there man."

"I know you will, young brother. I know you will."

"Randy."

"Yeah, young brother?"

"I ain't never told you this man, but you know I'm grateful to you, man. I'm grateful to you for slowing me down. I was stacking up years like a fool until I moved in here with you, man."

"I didn't do anything, young brother."

"It ain't what you did Randy, it was how you lived in this place man. How you carried yourself with respect. And I ain't talking about that loud demanding crap these others niggas be screaming about. I'm talking about the kind of respect you don't have to scream for. The kind that's given without demanding it. You was an example man and I would'a been a fool not to follow it. You found the pace of this place and following you, lead me to the pace. Man, I was beating my head against these walls until I slowed down with you and caught the pace. I owe you, man."

"No, no, young brother you don't owe me, you woulda caught the pace with or without me. But thank you, Cal."

Randolph knew that to be true because no one was an example for him and he caught the pace. The prison forced a pace on him. As a young man being of slight build, he came through the gates fighting for what he thought was his manhood. After it was taken, he found he remained a man; a man broken with shame and self pity. He was beaten and raped twice by the same three men. During the second rape he became a murderer.

He killed two of his attackers when the shank one held fell to the floor during the rape. Randolph recovered the knife and drove it into the rapist chest. The other he strangled, the third ran when he saw Randolph's shame and self-pity transformed into hate and vengeance. Randolph spent five years stalking the third attacker. It was a splintered ruler the guards found forced through his eye. They said his face was still screaming when they pulled his corpse from beneath the gym bleachers.

Calvin or none of the other inmates that arrived in the last ten years knew about the murders. The senior inmates and guards speculated, but the third rapist never confessed to raping Randolph, or identified him as the murderer of the other two.

"I'll see you in the morning, old folks."

"You sleep good, young fella."

Talking did ease Randolph's pain of wanting. In the darkness, in the space between his open eyes and the ceiling, he saw the Judge's soft pudgy face. The hate the rapist spawned in him didn't leave with their deaths. It festered in him. Randolph found in prison, festering hate was at home. His original six-year sentence increased as his hate found victims for unjustified vengeance. He beat a cell-mate for snoring, stabbed a man because the man called him cute and raped a man because others were raping him. When the raped man killed himself, Randolph's hate turned inward.

He tried to hang himself with electric wiring, it broke, he tried to poison himself by drinking laundry beach; the guards found him and pumped his stomach. He was shipped to the state mental hospital for thirty days. There he got to talk to a therapist everyday and he was given what he called 'feel good pills'. Although he talked to the therapist everyday, he didn't discuss how guilty he had felt about raping the young inmate, about how the young man's face had not left his mind during sleep, how he'd heard the young man's pleading whenever he'd sit quiet and alone. He didn't talk about these things with the therapist because the feel good pills stopped them from happening.

Two days after he started taking the pills he was able to sleep and didn't hear the young man's voice any more. It wasn't until he got back to the prison, minus the daily therapy sessions and minus the feel good pills that Randolph's guilt and hate overcame him. His first thought was to slam his head into the concrete wall to stop the maddening thoughts and sounds. He guessed the prison doctor must have seen something in his eyes during the check in because he immediately transferred him to the prison hospital and kept him sedated for a week.

Through the mushy reality the sedatives left him, he tried to blame someone for the chaos of his life. The only person he was able to focus on through the cloudiness of the drugs was the pudgy-faced Judge. He had sent Randolph to prison to become what he became.

When he left the prison hospital, his hate had weaved itself within every thought of the Judge. It was so intertwined with such depth and completeness within his thinking that Randolph's outside demeanor became calm. When he was released from the hospital, his outside pace was slower. His hate was busy inside his head, occupied with the Judge.

When the trial that got Randolph sent to prison first started, he found comfort in the softness of the Judge's pudgy face. The Judge sort of looked like Santa. Surely, Santa would see the truth he spoke. Surely, Santa's thick ears with red tips would filter the lies of the police from the truth. But it appeared that all Santa and the jury heard was that he'd been arrested twice before for selling marijuana, and each time he'd been given a break. The lady prosecutor said it was time to send a message to drug dealers.

When the lady prosecutor said drug dealer, Randolph looked around the courtroom for the drug dealer. He was certain she wasn't talking about him. He'd been arrested eight years ago for a quarter pound weed and was given community service. That didn't make him a drug dealer. Yes, he'd been arrested a couple of times. He was stopped by the police and they found the remains of a joints in his ashtray. He smoked weed. His ashtrays had the remains of joints in them, thereby his arrest record. He didn't sell weed. Yes, he knew where to get good weed, so he brought it and he and his friends split the cost. But that wasn't dope dealing and he'd been tried and convicted for that mistake.

He paid close attention to the words of the Judge that gave him the community service eight years ago and straighten out his life. He didn't stop smoking weed, but he stopped smoking in his car and he stopped buying for his friends. He was thirty-five years old at the time of his trial. He didn't make the same youthful mistakes. He had a good job at the mill, a beautiful wife and a son that looked like him. He was married man who was looking forward to married life.

The day Randolph got in trouble, he was giving a kid on the next block a jump. The kid gave him four bags of weed for his help. Driving around the corner home, he got stopped by the police, four bags qualified for distribution. In the eyes of the prosecutor he was a drug dealer.

Neither the Judge nor jury heard him or his lawyer. All they heard was Randolph's arrest record, a record that spanned over twenty years. It didn't concern them that he hadn't been arrested in eight years. They agreed with the prosecutor, drug dealers had to be punished. There were too many people in the jury to hate, but Randolph could hate the Judge. He could plan the Judge's death. The nightly thoughts that he had before he went to sleep were of women and varied sexual acts. After the Judge took center stage in his thinking; plans of the Judge's death were the thoughts that lead him to sleep. Fire bombing the Judge's court with a forty-ounce bottle full of gas was his favorite thought before sleep. The Judge's robes would catch a flame and he'd fling himself through a window screaming in agony. Another favorite was kidnapping the Judge and torturing him hourly; grate a patch of skin from his body, drive a nail through a tooth, place leeches on his tongue, and feed him oatmeal with ground glass. These were the ideas the lead him to sleep until six months ago. Then he heard of the Judge's recent practice of meeting the men he'd sentenced at the dispatch gate and shaking their hands.

At the gate when the Judge put his hand in Randolph's, the plan was to pull the Judge in close, and choke the life out of him. It was said the Judge was old and frail and could barely shake a man's hand. Randolph was old, but he wasn't frail. He knew his strength would hold even if a guard's bullet found his head.

Every night for six months the thought was the same, choke the Judge, choke the life from him no matter what. He visualized himself riddled with bullets, but his hands remained around the Judge's neck. Although he was told age had withered the Judge, in his minds eye the Judge's face remained pudgy and round. And it was the pudgy round face that Randolph saw wanting and pleading for life. It was the pudgy round face that Randolph denied life.

Randolph wasn't spry the next morning spry when he woke up. His knees where stiff and his neck was rigid, because of these ailments he was slow getting to the shower. His usual hot shower was cold. Calvin and a couple of other inmates pitched in and brought him a suit, a shirt and a pair of shoes from outside the prison. The clothes were shipped to the warden, so he allowed Randolph to change from his prison issue into the new suit in his bathroom.

Randolph liked the suit, the pants were loose fitting and the jacket was a single breasted two button with slit pockets. The gray wool laid good on his shoulders. He turned and faced himself in the warden's bathroom mirror.

"Damn boy, you still a good looking brother when you clean your-self up. Might be some help for you yet."

His own smile made him smile more. Damn, if he wasn't happy at the sight of himself.

Outside his knees loosened up on the walk to the gate. The leather soles of his new loafers slapped the pavement. It had been decades since he worn leather soles, rubber was on the bottom of the prison boots. The warden was saying something to him, but it didn't regis-ter, it was bright day and he was wondering would the sunlight hold until the inmates got called to yard.

He noticed the warden had fallen behind a step and was hustling to keep up with him. Randolph laughed, he hadn't out-walked any-one years. His prison pace seldom required a fast step, but he wasn't walking at a prison pace. He didn't slow down for the warden.

He stretched out his arm and brought his wrist up and checked the time. The cuff of his new white shirt covered half of his old Timex. It was 10:35a.m. his release time was 10:30a.m. He was behind sched-ule. He'd brought the wind up Timex when he got hired at the steel mill forty years ago. When he got to the prison, a guard took it from him. He thought it was gone forever, thirty-eight years wasn't forever.

The watch was still ticking, and so was he. The Timex was his only remaining possession from life before prison. In those days he'd set it fifteen minutes ahead of the mill's time clock, he hated being late for work. Today he set it by the warden's watch.

The steel mill paid him well. He brought nice suits when he worked. He liked wearing nice suites and he liked his job at the mill. He liked the suit he was wearing now. He liked the pace he was walking and he liked the fact that the warden couldn't keep up with him.

He dropped his arm when he got to the dispatch gate. The warden caught up to Randolph and gave him an envelope to give the guard. He shook Randolph's hand and told him life was waiting for him outside the gate.

The handshake changed Randolph's chipper mood. For a short time he hadn't thought about the Judge's death. For a short time he thought about wearing nice suits. For a short time he thought about life before prison. Randolph passed the envelope through the gate to the guard. The guard opened the envelope, waved his hand, and the gate opened.

He stepped across the gate tracks and took his first free breath in thirty-eight years. He wasn't smiling; he wasn't laughing; he was merely breathing. Two steps away Randolph saw an aged man. The face was smaller, but it was Santa, and he had a huge helper with him. Beyond the aged Judge and his bodyguard Randolph saw two other men, two Black men.

One was a slender man in a good suit and his stance was familiar to Randolph. He stood like Randolph's remembered his own father standing—way back on his knees. The other man was only a large boy, but he too was familiar.

The bodyguard began to explain to Randolph why he and the Judge where there, but Randolph walked past the Judge's extended hand. His head was suddenly filled with the scent of rose water.

"Are you Randolph Parker?" the man asked as Randolph approached them.

The boy said nothing; his eyes were cast down.

"Yes." Randolph answered. "I am Randolph Parker."

"I am Raymond Parker . . . and I thought you was dead. . . . My mama, bless her soul, told me you were dead when I was boy. That old man behind you came to see me last week and told me my daddy was getting released from prison. I told him he was crazy, my daddy was dead, but I came anyway and I brought my son . . . my son . . . I brought my son to see his grandfather . . . just in case it was true . . . just in case . . . my daddy . . . was alive. This here is my son, . . . Randolph Parker."

The three Parker men stood silent with only two looking at each other.

Randolph felt a tap on his shoulder. He glanced over his shoulder and saw the Judge.

"Mr. Parker. I like to tell you your debt to society has been paid, don't let anyone tell you different." The Judge placed his hand firmly on Randolph's shoulder and continued with his head lowered in prayer; "May God bless you and keep you in his grace always, amen."

Randolph eyes were intently on the Judges knotted, liver spotted fingers. He turned and faced the Judge. The Judge extended his hand and Randolph shook it.

"Thank you for telling my son about me." He released the Judge's hand and turned back to his son and grandson. A son. A grandson. A son and a grandson. Having them in Randolph's life was a gift from God, yes, but it was also a gift from the judge. That gift gave Randolph his life back. They stood again silent.

Then, the grandson, who Randolph noticed was not dressed well, but in oversized clothes said, "Well, you gonna drive him home, Daddy, or what? I'm tried of standing in front of a prison No offense . . . um . . . Granddaddy, but this ain't a comfortable place for a young Black man to be standing, and I know you ain't too happy about standing around here. So let's ride Daddy, like the white man said, "It's paid fo".

10

Old Folks' Home

You know, a neighborhood can break your heart. This one here now broke mine enough fo' two life times. That's one reason I'm movin'. A person my age feels a heartbreak. One would think that gettin' older would lessen the pain, but that is not how it's been for me. I feel every heartbreak.

I am going to miss sitting out here on my porch in the evening though, but I now already talked to the nice little half-colored half-Chinese real estate lady. She found two good places for me and I been approved for both of them. They both got balconies big enough for this old rocker. I won't see the same folks, but I will still be able to sit out and rock in my granddaddy's chair. I just have to make up my mind on which place to call home out of the two she found.

Lord, there goes Tyrel, that was a fine car he's drivin'. It ain't worth spit now. His daddy gave it to him maybe ten, twelve years ago. If you ask me, that was the biggest mistake his daddy made; other than drinkin' whiskey with the boy.

Now Tyrel is definitely one of my heartbreaks. The boy had promise, smart as a whip, but he thought bein' cool on the street was better than bein' smart in school. Soon, as his daddy gave him that car them "good timein" fools pulled him into they crowd. I don't like that word much . . . fool, but there ain't nothin' else to call some people. They didn't have nothin' and didn't want him to have anythin'. Misery loves company.

All they wanted was somebody to drive them around. They showed that schoolboy the fast life and turned him around good. The boy ain't looked up from whiskey, drugs and loose woman yet. I tried to talk to him, and tell him that he wasn't cut out fo' the streets but he thought like most young people; that old folks don't know squat. Ain't nothing new under the sun, but these young kids don't know that.

And now Tyrel livin' off his mama and me and drinkin' more than his daddy ever did. The boy did finish high school, but he cain't seem to keep a job. And he has a good head fo' figures. I let him do my taxes every year and he gets me a little money back. He just got to learn that workin' and drinkin' don't mix. Matter of fact he got to learn that him and drinkin' don't mix.

He gets dressed up every Friday night and goes to that bucket of blood around the corner. Now that's another reason I'm movin', the place use to be a decent neighborhood bar. It ain't nothin' now but a place fo' our young colored boys to stand in front of and wait fo' trouble.

You know I loves my colored people, but I show am gettin' tired of seein' them standin' and sittin' around. My daddy use to tell me to look busy even if I wasn't. "Ain't nothin worst than a triflin' man' he said." Well, this neighborhood is full of them. And Lord as my witness I'm tired of seein' them. I wants to come outside and sit in my granddaddy's rocker and not see one colored person standin' around doin' nothin'.

I think the sixties made some colored people lazy. Made them think white folks thought of them as equals, so they didn't have to work twice as hard no mo'. Damn fools, as far as I'm concerned a colored person always got to do double. That's just the way of this white man's world.

Well, the new places that girl showed me ain't got no lazy colored people standin' around. They got a few coloreds, but they coloreds with good jobs, like this neighborhood use to have. These young fools sittin' around here on porches forgot, or don't know how hard they grandparents worked to get these houses. They sittin' on them porches drinkin' and peein' in the corners. Now what kind of sense does that make, peein' in the corner of you're own porch? They ain't got the sense they was born with.

Joanne shoulda been back with my numbers and my Coca Cola. I played some new numbers today. I played the addresses of the places that nice colored China doll showed me. I ain't too old to change my ways of doin' things. I likes to switch my lottery numbers sometimes. Change is good every now and then.

That's another reason I'm movin' to a new neighborhood. I needs me some change, somethin' new in my life. New things perk up a tired mind, leaning and doing somethin' new keeps the mind growin'. A growin' mind is a healthy mind.

I didn't give Joanne enough money to run off with although she said she would never do that again. Like my Daddy said 'once bitten twice shy'. Yeah, she was sorry, but sorry didn't pay my light bill that month. Love the girl like my own child, but I never give her more than three dollars to go to the store with. No sirree Bob.

Joanne got to be fifty if she's a day. Always got a couple of young fellows keepin' her company, but soon as they get wise to her turnin'-money-to-smoke ways, they leave her alone. If I had somethin' to do me as bad as that stuff now done her, I'd ask the good Lord to take me on away from here. Well, maybe not, the sweet Lord don't put nothin' on you you cain't handle. And Lord knows us colored people done been through it.

That crack stuff just somethin' else for use to go through. 'The gift is in the struggle' my daddy use to say. We'll get through this crack mess just like we got through slavery and Jim Crow. It ain't nothin' but some mo' mess to keep us down. Watch us get by it. Just like everythin' else.

It breaks my heart to see Joanne like she is, but I know she will get better. Last week I saw her straighten out her clothes before she came up on my porch. That's a good sign, she startin' to care again about how she looks.

Her mama left that house to her, but now Joanne's ex-husband and his new wife and family live upstairs. She lives downstairs in that damp basement and she got asthma. I remember when she had her first attack as a baby. My daddy had the only car on the block, so him, me and her mama carried her to the hospital. Seein' such a little thing that sick scared me good. I stayed with her and her mama the whole night at the hospital. After we brought her home, she might as well had been my child the way I kept an eye on her and been watchin' her every since.

I brought her high school prom dress. I sent her money when she went off to college and picked her up from the airport after she flunked out. I went to see her off when she joined the U.S. Air Force. I danced real good at her weddin'. I helped bury her mama and her daddy after the car accident. Lord, that was a sad day.

Some folks around here say her mama and daddy dyin' caused her to start messin' with that crack mess, but I don't know that to be true. Joanne was always a curious girl. If you ask me, that's what got her started, wantin' to see what is was like. I thank the good Lord fo' my simple mind. I ain't curious about too much of nothin'.

Well, I must admit I am curious to see how this new crop of grown up coloreds goin' to turn out, the ones that went away to college and finished. The ones that old folks like me say got 'good jobs'; the one's we brag on.

Shoot, they moved out of here so fast I can hardly remember them. Looks like to me they went away to college and never came back. I see pictures of their kids playin' in big yards with white kids, but I don't see them. They seldom come back to the neighborhood. Their folks go way out there to their houses. Maybe colored neighborhoods are a thing of the past. It might be safer for us to mix all up with other folks. Jamal put that thought in my head.

Jamal was always talkin' about white folks tryin' to kill all the colored people. He said we was stupid for livin' in one place. That boy had a hundred different ways the white folks was goin' to use to kill us. They was goin' to poison the water they sent to colored neighorhoods or they was goin' to cut off the trucks that brought food to colored neighborhoods. Oh, he could talk all night about it. He talked so much he scared himself. Maybe that's why he married that white woman and moved way out there where they ain't got no street lights and no other colored folk but him.

He broke my heart when he did that because I expected him to be a leader. Everybody did, we all sat around listenin' to him. Now, if he got us to listen, he could have got a lot of other colored folks to listen. I guess that one white woman listenin' is enough for him.

Maybe, if them young grown up coloreds with they good jobs and college education came back and brought up these empty lots and built some new houses this would be a nice colored neighborhood again. You know education spreads. One smart colored person can help a whole heap of colored folks. Look at Oprah.

You know, that would be somethin' if they did come back. Ohwee! I get excited thinkin' about it. It would be like old times, us helpin' us. Only better because mo' of us is educated. You know young children follow what they see. Suppose these young children around here had a block full of educated colored folks to follow behind: instead of what they got now.

Think of how a social worker, teacher, doctor or lawyer livin next do' would help these young children. Yes siree Bob, that would sho' nuff beat this crack mess, stop it from gettin' new curious minds. I show hope I live long enough to see it.

You know, if you think about it, that's only part of what's missin' from our neighborhoods—young colored folks with good jobs and education. The other part is old folks like me. We runnin' out to nice, safe neighborhoods and forgettin' our wisdom is needed. Old folks spent time with young children in my day. Watched over us and warned us about life, told us things to look out fo' and swatted our butts with tree switches when we got out of line.

The first time I heard about Burr Rabbit I was sttin' in old folks laps. You know I ain't told none of these children around here one story. I could have, they always playin' around my steps. Well, if I wasn't movin', I might start.

Ain't goin' to be no mo' coloreds neighborhoods. Folks movin' were they feel safe and I cain't blame them. You suppose to feel safe at home. I use to feel safe in this neighborhood, sittin' in old folks laps.

I guess I could tell a couple of them one Burr Rabbit story befo' I move. You know, a neighborhood can break your heart.

11

Mama and Santa Claus

My mama told me a long time ago it wasn't no Santa Claus. Some of the kids at the Home Center think it is a Santa Claus. Especially, Richard, he believes in Santa a lot and will beat any kid who says there ain't a Santa. I wish, I hope, I want to believe that there is a Santa, but my mama told me there ain't no Santa Claus.

Last Christmas I was staying at the Larkin's home. Mr. and Mrs. Larkin and they kids believe in Santa and, while I was there, I believed too because he came to they house. Everybody got presents! I got three, a personal CD player, a pair of gym shoes and a yellow dump truck was all under the dressed up Christmas tree. Three wrapped up gifts with my name on the tags, they said 'To Anthony from Santa'.

I wouldn't have mind staying at the Larkin's, but I couldn't because they home is only a temporary site; at least that's what the social worker said. I think the reason I didn't stay was because of my burned hand. It scared they little boy, Justin. My hand is scary. I try to keep it in my pocket, so it won't scare the little kids at the Home Center. Justin saw it while we was opening presents and he started crying. I tried to hide it afterwards but it was too late. I didn't mean to mess up the little boy's Christmas. I had to come back the Home Center that afternoon. But they did let me keep the presents Santa brought me.

I really wasn't sad about coming back to Home Center because the very next day the kids from our ward went on a trip to the zoo. We were having fun up until we got the ape house. When we got there, Richard pointed to a gorilla's hand and said it looked like mine.

The guide worker told him animals didn't have hands; they have claws. In front of the gorilla cage Richard turned to me and said, "You don't have a hand; you got a claw."

He and the other kids thought that was funny and started laughing until I took the silver top off the concrete ashtray and knocked him upside the head with it. Wasn't nobody laughing then because they thought the zoo trip was going to be over. Any fights break out, we go back to the Home Center. But the guide worker had walked to the other cage, so he didn't see me hit Richard upside his fat head.

Richard is the biggest kid in our ward at the Home Center. He is a bully, but he don't mess with me anymore cause he know I ain't scared of him. So, today when he started slapping kids who said it wasn't no Santa Claus, he didn't even come my way. I know why he slapping kids. He's like me; he wants to believe in Santa because it would be better if it was a Santa Claus. He wants to believe that Santa is going to come to the Home Center and leave us presents under the naked Christmas tree the staff put up.

I want to believe that too. At first when I was at the Larkin's, I didn't believe in Santa because my mama had told me it wasn't no such thing as Santa Claus. But being around the Larkin's six kids that did believe, made me want to believe. Mr. and Mrs. Larkin believed and they are gown ups. So, that night at the Larkin's I went to sleep thinking it might be a Santa Claus. The next morning I woke up and I had presents under the tree.

Everybody at the Larkin's home believed in Santa and he came to they house. It makes sense that everybody in a place have to believe if they want Santa to come. That's why Richard is slapping kids upside the head. He wants everybody to believe, so we can all get toys from Santa. I guess the toys and stuff we get at the Home Center for Christmas is not enough for him.

Yesterday we lined up for a bunch of toys from a church. They hand four tables of toys and we could pick whatever we wanted. The toys were all new and I am happy with mine. I got a real leather basketball. So what, if it wasn't wrapped up and under a tree. Something is better than nothing. Today we watched Christmas movies all day and kids got to talking about Santa Claus and magic. Richard wants the magic and he thinks if anybody doesn't believe, the magic won't happen.

It's the same with getting a placement out of the Home Center, the social workers always to tell us to believe it will happen and it will happen. I am eight years old and I have been here since I was five. What I know is that babies and real little kids get placed. Older kids like me go to group homes. Don't none of that matter to me because I going back home with my mama anyway. As soon as she gets better and the head doctor says she can take care of me without hurting me, we going to move back to our place.

I don't have to make myself believe in Santa because my mama is getting better and she going to take me out of here. And she told me ain't no Santa Claus. I kinda wish Richard would come over and ask me what I think. I would set him straight right away. Ain't no Santa and his big butt ain't go get placed and ain't no kind of magic around the Home Center. Tomorrow morning is Christmas and when he wakes up, it's going to oatmeal, scrambled eggs, sausages, juice and toast for breakfast. No special Christmas breakfast like in the movies. The naked Christmas tree will still be in the day-area in the middle of the eating tables until staff takes it down. Richard can slap as many kids upside the head as he wants, but that still isn't going to change a thing around here and it ain't going to make Santa Claus real. This ain't "A Miracle on 34th Street" this is the Home Center and ain't no magic. This ain't the movies. Santa Claus don't come here.

But . . . if Santa was real like at the Larkin's, I would ask him to make my mama better, so we could go back to our place and be like we use to be before she burnt my hand. I would ask him to bring Richard and every kid in here, a present with they name on it. That's a good feeling to get a present from Santa with your own name on it, and I think all the kids in here would like that.

Ms. Mildred, the lady who cooks our dinner, brought us all butter cookies after lights out. She came to each of our beds and gave us a cookie and a kiss on the cheek and told us Merry Christmas. She won't be here tomorrow because she got to fly down South to see her parents who are getting up in age. I was going to save my cookie for in the morning. I'm getting sleepy and think, if I go to sleep, I might roll over on it and crush it or Richard might sneak over and take it while I am asleep, So, I eat it and go to sleep.

Santa Claus never came to me and mama's place because mama didn't believe and told me not to believe. I wonder if Richard slapped enough kids into believing, to make Santa come by here tonight while we sleeping. I hope my mama has a good Christmas, I don't know if a church will bring people at the head hospital presents or not.

I would ask Santa to fix my hand because it does look like a animal claw, but I know that's too big a thing to ask from him, I just hope he brings the real little kids some toys because they really believe. I hope he brings my mama something too because, if he brought her something when she didn't believe, she might start believing. It worked that way for me. I think I do believe in Santa Claus, but I don't think he's going to stop by here, but I hope he does.

At first I thought I was smelling the my cookie from last night, but after I got all the way woke, I knew it wasn't a cookie. It is a sweet cake-like smell that has filled the whole ward. Every kid is smelling it. We are all up and running into the day area.

The first thing I see is the naked tree. It ain't naked no more! It's all dressed up with a white star on the top and gold trimming and sliver icy looking things and red and green balls and little dolls and real candy canes and strings and strings of popcorn. It's a movie Christmas tree!

On the eating tables are big plates filled with stacks of pancakes and slices of ham and baskets with bread rolls, there is bottles of syrup and jars of jelly, there is bowls of cheese eggs and bowls grits with butter, there is bacon and sausages and fruits. But what makes us kids stop is the mountain of presents under the now dressed up tree.

Staff is standing against the windows just looking at us and the mountain of gifts. Mr. Raymond, the boss, walks between us and the gifts. He calls me and Richard out; he says we are to be his helpers. He's going to call names of kids and we got to take them they presents from Santa.

Every kid's name gets called five times, but couldn't nobody open a present until we ate breakfast. You talking about kids eating good food fast. We ain't doing nothing, but laughing and chewing. Even the staff sits at our tables and eats with us. It is both daytime staff and nighttime staff and everybody is happy.

Richard just keeps saying, "I told y'all he was gonna come, I told y'all!" He did tell us; he kept believing. I can't stop looking at the tree. It's got little elves and little tiny Santa Clauses all over it. But what's even better than the tree to me is that everybody's present got name tags with they names and 'from Santa'. Now everybody knows he is real.

I was so busy eating and looking at everything and everybody I didn't see the church choir come in. I just heard them once they started singing the Christmas songs. Man, it's like the movies for real.

Staff cleared the eating tables and let us open our gifts right there. I was thinking that all us kids was gonna have the same things, but we all got different gifts. I got colored markers and a sketch pad, a remote control racing car, a big chocolate bar, a Play Station football game and a picture frame with a picture of my mama in it! This is the best Christmas ever! And that's for real. I am going to always believe in Santa Claus! Always.

PART TWO

"A Lil' Twisted"

I

Brotherly Love

It was once a beautiful sun porch. In it's day breezes could be felt from the east, the west and the north. The house faces the north. It was said his great, great grandfather built it facing north because he found comfort in gazing upon the North Star. Family legend says he followed it up from Mississippi to his freedom.

Currently, no eastern or west winds blow through the sun porch. The east and west window screens were replaced with plywood. The only screen on the porch is the half screen in the security door. Glass blocks have replaced the screens that once faced north.

Behind the glass blocks in an old wicker chair atop the loose floorboards of the porch sits Simon Johnson. Simon or Slim as his neighbors call him is in his first good mood in over five years. His last good mood came during his senior year in high school; the night of homecoming. He was the manager of the football team and after the home coming victory the players invited him out to drink. For the first time they treated him like a player instead of the towel boy. It was a good night for Slim.

Today's good mood however outweighs the one of yesteryear by a landslide. Slim's good mood today is in response to a check for one hundred and fifty thousand dollars. The accompanying letter explains the check as payment on a life insurance policy from his father's death. He wasn't aware that his wayward father had died, but the news of his death didn't stop the good mood brought on by the check.

For the past two hours Slim sat in the old wicker chair grinning at the check. One hundred fifty thousand dollars could make right so much that is wrong in his life. This much money could free him of the responsibility his mother left him with.

The first thing he would do if he could get free would be to move to Chicago and get lost among the hundreds of thousands of people that live there. He wouldn't need much living by himself, only a one-bedroom apartment in a neighborhood with a busy nightlife. He knew how to live fugally. He had learn that this past four years and, besides, there had to be many janitorial, restaurant and or carwash jobs in the city. All he would need would be a little income to supplement his windfall.

The big city is the place for guy like himself, a quiet guy who minds his own business. Twice a year for the past two years he has been able to slip away to Chicago for weekend stays, thanks to the consideration of his lifetime neighbors.

Two years ago an elderly Mr. and Mrs. Langston suggested that he let his brother stay with them for two weekends out of a year.

"It's the least we could do, Slim," Mrs. Langston had said. "We suggested the same thing to your mother, but she was a dedicated soul and wouldn't leave your bother's side."

Slim didn't hesitate to accept the offer. On these weekend trips he rents a transient hotel room in the red light district. He spends his weekend with the first prostitute that approaches him. He is grateful for the assertiveness these city women display because, if it was left to him to speak first, his needs would go unmet.

The alarm on his wristwatch is beeping; three and a half hours have passed since Jesse's last cleaning and changing. Slim looks down at the stack of freshly powdered adult diapers that he keeps on the side of the wicker chair. He usually responds quickly to beep of the watch but today . . . he just stares at the stack of diapers with the insurance check between his fingers.

Slim looks down at the check; Jesse's name is not on it. The check reads 'Pay to the order of Simon Johnson'. No mention of his brother, Jesse Johnson. He had not thought of Jesse when he thought of moving to Chicago because Jesse was the reason he couldn't move there or anywhere else. His brother has been in his sole care for the past three years since their mother's death. Before her death, her life revolved around his younger bother. Now Slim felt his life revolved him.

His father left two years after Jesse was born. Slim was eight years old. He remembers the day clearly. He was sitting on the bottom step of the sun porch waiting on his mother to take him to church. His mother had spent the morning fussing about his father not coming home the previous night. His father pulled up to the curb in his white Pontiac and called him over. Slim ran from the step to his father hoping for a ride to church in the new car.

"Boy," his father said, "you my son. I don't know what that thang is in the house yo mama be dotin' over. All I knows is you is mine and I'ma always take care of you. See ya around, boy." After that day he only saw his father on his birthdays and Christmas. And after tenth grade he never saw him again.

Slim folded the check and slipped into his shirt pocket. He reached down grabbed a powdered diaper. Jesse's room is at the rear of the house across from the bathroom exactly sixteen steps from where he stood. He knew the exact amount of steps because out of boredom he often made the trip with his eyes closed.

He'd anchored Jesse in the armchair earlier. His mother didn't like him to tie Jesse to chairs, but Slim tied him down for safety. If Jesse's back wasn't secured, he would lean over. Slim had brought the armchair in from the living room and put it next to Jesse's bed.

Jesse's life in Slim's care was spent either in the bed, in the tub or in the chair. Occasionally, Slim would take him out to sit on the sun pouch or to the front yard. As far as Slim could tell Jesse couldn't tell the difference from the sun porch or the tub. The same inanimate expression would remain on his face.

A doctor once told his mother that there was a fifteen percent chance that Jesse would respond to stimuli later in life. Because of that fifteen percent chance she refused to put him in a home. "The good Lord can work with fifteen percent" was her quiet chant. It was this small hope that caused her to make Slim promise not to put Jesse in a home. Today with his mother dead and the check in his pocket the promise seems minor.

For years Slim had wondered what were the real chances of Jesse ever responding to anything and, if he did respond, what would it be—a flinch to a rub? When Slim entered Jesse's bedroom, he notices the light on the dehumidifier blinking. The unit is on the side of the bed one first sees when entering the room. Slim reaches down and pulls the bucket from the bottom of the unit. He steps across the hall to the bathroom and dumps the water in the toilet. His mother was wrong; Jesse belonged in a home. Back in the room he slides the bucket into place. The dehumidifier hums on.

Even the home-aide nurse that comes once a week told Slim that Jesse's care would be better in a home. In a home he would see a doctor weekly and, certainly, a doctor would notice signs of improvement before Slim. Slim agreed, but the home cost was beyond what his mother left in trust for him and Jesse. Even with state aide Slim would be expected to kick in six to eight hundred dollars a month for a home and he simply couldn't afford it before the check. Now with the check he doesn't want to afford it.

This check was from his father for him and the one thing he was certain of is that it was all going to spent by him on him. He tossed the diaper on the bed and walk around to Jesse. This morning Slim had dressed Jesse exactly like himself in a pair of gray sweat shorts, a tee shirt and a pair of thick socks. He slid his hand into the shorts and down the back of Jesse's diaper. It was dry.

"Darn it. Sorry about that, Jessie." He forgot to give him his afternoon fluids. The squeeze container is still on the nightstand full. He grabs it from the stand and leans Jesse's head back. He slides the tube gently to the back of Jesse's mouth and slightly squeezes the container.

Watching the fluid line he says, "No. I can't afford to send you to the home." Slim lowers the container and pulls the tube from Jesse's mouth. Looking at his brother's face, he sees his mother. She spent her life taking care of Jesse. "Not me, Mom. I can't." He tightened the knots on the chair straps and walks back up front to the sun porch.

He sits in the wicker chair and the loose floorboards of the porch creak. He pulls the insurance check from his shirt pocket. One hundred fifty thousand dollars this was less than what was left in trust to him and Jesse by their mother, but it is windfall nonetheless. The trust, suppose the trust and the check was all his, then, he could live well in the city without working a menial job. He sat back in the chair and imagined it so.

He saw himself walking down a busy city street dressed in a flowing white linen outfit. Even dressed well, he still waited for the prostitutes to approach him. The ones that approached him were voluptuous and curvaceous. Instead of taking them to a small transient hotel room, he took them to a hotel suite complete with a whirlpool bath and champagne on ice. It was a rap music video that played in his mind and he was the star. He no longer drove the station wagon his mother left him; in his minds eye he had a new SUV with twenty-four inch chrome rims. With the trust and the check, he could make a lot happen. Maybe, he couldn't buy a new SUV because a new SUV cost as much as what their house was appraised for, but even a two-year-old one would be better than the station wagon.

The house. Slim sat up in the wicker chair. The house was appraised for seventy thousand dollars. If Jesse was in a home and he moved to the city, they wouldn't need the house. He could sell it and the station wagon. If he sold the house and took only half the trust, he could afford to put Jesse in a home and move to the city. Freedom was possible. Slim stood from the wicker chair smiling. A life where he was only responsible for himself could be had. He put the check back in his shirt pocket and went back to Jesse's room.

In the corner of the room next to the closet is Jesse's wheel chair. Slim hadn't had Jesse on the sun porch or sitting in the front yard for a long time. Today he suddenly felt like being outside in the yard with his brother. He transferred Jesse from the armchair to the wheelchair easily. He doesn't bother to strap Jessie into the wheel chair. His thoughts are on the check, selling the house and the whole trust fund. What if all this was his?

When Slim opens the door of the sun porch, he sees Mr. and Mrs. Langston out on their porch enjoying the evening air. They wave. Slim returns their waves and shouts, "Evening."

Mrs. Langston returns the greeting, "Good evening, Slim. It's good to see Jesse out."

"Yes ma'am, I thought he might like to catch the last of summer. We're going to sit in the yard a while." He shouts across the road.

Usually, Slim wouldn't leave Jesse sitting in the doorway of the sun porch, but today he let him sit at the top of the stairs. Usually, he would engage the brake on the wheel of the chair, but today he doesn't push down on the lever that digs into the rubber wheel of the chair.

Today, he is thinking of a two year old SUV, white linen clothes, music video females and a whole trust fund.

Usually, Slim would never walk away from the chair leaving Jesse sitting at the top of the stairs, but today he does. And usually, he would never step on the end of the lose plank by the door because it would causes the other end of the plank to rise, the end at the top of the stairs. Today his foot rests on the plank. Mrs. Langston screams before Slim does.

Slim makes a frantic effort to grab the handles of the wheel chair, but the chair with un-engaged brakes rolls quickly once the plank rose up. There are two flights of stairs leading up to the Johnson sun porch. Jesse remained seated the first six steps of the top flight, but the slightly wider step at the beginning the second flight toppled his chair and sent him tumbling twisted down the last six steps. It wasn't until his head got to the pavement that his wheel chair forced his body over to an angle that caused his neck to snap.

The snap is heard all the way across road by Mr. and Mrs.Langston who are hurrying to Jesse's aid. Slim has slung the wheel chair aside and is on his knees next to his brother. Mr. Langston is behind him "Don't move him, Slim! Emily go on in and call ambulance!"

Slim checks for Jesse pulse and feels none. His hand goes from his brother's wrist to patting his own shirt pocket for the check. It's still in place. It's not his brother he sees twisted at the bottom of the sun porch steps, but his freedom. The tear he sheds is not a sad tear.

2

The Finishing Place

He paces the high edge of the rooftop slowly. It is a clear night with a bright moon. His decision was made before he climbed the five flights of stairs. He paces simply to pace. The street below is busy; but no one has looked up. He thinks he will go unnoticed until his body splatters on the pavement below. He inhales the crisp night air deeply as he crouches for his leap.

From the shadows comes, "Hey! Hey there!"

He ignores the call. This task has to be completed. His death is the only way to end turmoil.

"Hey, boy, I'm talking to ya! What is ya? Another one of dem crackheads 'bout to kill yaself? Damn! Two of y'all jumped last week. I wish y'all would find another place fo' dat shit. Why all y'all want to die anyway? I mean as much as y'all seem to enjoy dat mess seems to me like y'all would want to stay alive and smoke some mo'. What. . . is death part of da high?"

Deacon slowly turns from the street and looks into the darkness of the rooftop. He sees no one. His skinny malnourished body shifts on the ledge and leans forward.

"Where are you? Show yourself."

"Why? Ya don't need to see me. Lord knows I didn't need to see yo ass. Go on and finish what ya started crack-head. Pay me no mind."

"What? What did you call me? Hey, fuck you, man!"

"Ya too late. I'm already fucked."

Deacon Anderson jumps from the high ledge to the rooftop with his eyes searching the blackness, he wants to find the voice. The streetlights are beneath the roof and their beams shine down to the street. The only light on the roof is from the moon.

"Where are you?"

"I'm nowhere and everywhere crackhead."

"Stop calling me that!"

"Why? Dat's what ya is ain't it ?"

Deacon says nothing. The voice is right. A crackhead is all that he is.

"I was more once."

"But cha ain't now."

"No, I'm not now." He backs up and leans against the waist high brick ledge. He looks up to the clear night sky instead of the shadows of the roof. "I'm not now." He says softly.

"What? What cha say crackhead?"

"I said your right. I am a crackhead. I'm just another crackhead trying to end it."

"Tryin' to end it huh? So, I was right, killin' yaself is part of da high."

"Yeah, I guess so."

"Damn! Dat must be some good shit."

"What?"

"Dat crack, it must be good."

Suddenly exhausted; Deacon slumps his narrow shoulders, "What do you want, man? Why are you here?"

There wasn't to be anyone to witness his demise. His death was to be a clean and quick; a simple step into the night. He realizes now that he shouldn't have paced, the pacing gave the voice time to speak. If he would have jumped when he first got to the rooftop, it would all be over. The misery would have ended.

"I got business up here same as you crackhead. And what I want is fo' ya not to jump."

"Why? You don't know me. You couldn't possible care if I live or die. What does my jumping have to do with you?"

"If ya jump, folks will come around here, dey will keep dis place busy for a day or so. I don't care if you jump, just don't do it here."

"You don't care? Don't you have concern for a human life?"

"Ya ain't human! You a crackhead. Y'all walk around da streets like zombies. Takin' whatever ya can. A bunch of fuckin' rats. Naw, I don't give a fuck about cha, cause ya don't give a fuck about yaself. Shit, the truth be known I wish all y'all would die. None of ya deserve da life the Good Lord gave ya."

The voice summed up Deacon's own feeling about himself and it upset him. It is was one thing for him to feel that away about himself, but it was an entirely different matter to hear someone else say such things about him. For the voice to verbalize it sparks a little anger within him.

"Who the fuck are you, a judge from the shadows? Who are you to wish death on someone else? You're nothing but an old tired voice from the darkness; an old tired wino type voice. That's what you are a wino! And probably a disgusting one, one so nasty and filthy you're afraid to show yourself. That's why you slither in the pissy shadows of darkness. You're just as worthless and fucked up as I am. Isn't that right, isn't that right, wino?"

The rooftop is absent of voices.

"Yeah, I know you. Why so quiet, piss mongrel; Lavish Lord of Shityness? Have you nothing to say? No, I think not. Perhaps you care to join me on the ledge? After all you said it yourself, you're fucked. Come on wino . . . let's jump together! The crackhead and the wino; I'm sure there is a social statement in there somewhere. It will be our victory over life's cruelty. Together, wino, we beat life. Come from the shadows, my disgusting peer."

Deacon hears the gulping of someone taking a drink. He laughs out loud, "Sent you to your bottle didn't I?"

"What was ya crackhead? A teacher, a social worker, a writer. What was ya befo' ya turned into to nothin'? Sounds like ya mighta been smart. So, why don't cha take yo smart ass somewhere else and jump? Ya ain't wanted here. Dis is my place. Go on, get!"

"Fuck you. I go where I want and do what I want."

"Naw, you go were crack want and do what crack say."

"Look, old man. I'm going to tell you this just once. Get off the roof and mind your own business! If you don't go on your own, I'm going to throw you off this motherfucker! Stay alive old man and hit the stairs."

"Crackhead ya take one step toward me and I'll cut cha from asshole to appetite. Ya want to be a stupid mothafucker and jump off of dis roof; ya go head on. You right, I shouldna said shit to ya worthless ass. So, pretend like I ain't here and go on, finish what ya started. Go on, finish ya high, boy!"

"What? You're going to watch?"

"Shit! Why not? I ain't doing nothing else. Just sittin' here drankin'. Might as well enjoy da show. Go on, boy, jump!"

"That's probably what you've done your whole life; sit, drink and watch. You wino-ass motherfucker!"

"Yeap, I spend a lot of time watching dumb shit; but cha crack-heads, y'all always give me somethin' to watch. Y'alls da dumbest mothafuckers I ever watched. Just runnin' up and down da street, back and forth, back and forth until all ya money is gone. None of ya mothafuckers sit still. Y'all like, like, like . . . roaches! I wish all y'all would die. Jump, mothafucker!"

Neither the voice, nor Deacon spoke. After a quiet minute Deacon asks, "Who do you know that is a crackhead?"

"None of ya mothafuckin' business!"

"You love them; don't you? Who is it, one of your children? Who? What crack-head hurt you, maybe a young girl? Was she a sweet young thing? Did she take all your money? Did you trust her? Did you hope she would stop? What crack-head hurt you wino?"

"Shut da fuck up!"

"Damn wino. It was a pretty young thing. Did she make you feel alive? Did she cook your dinner and keep your wine cold? Was she good company? Did it hurt you to find out she loved crack more than you? Were you an old fool wino? Don't feel bad wino . . . you never stood a chance."

Deacon was overcome with the memory of all the pain he caused his own trusting wife and mother. He began to weep. They believed in him once, believed he could stop using the drug and return to the man he was, but he and they were wrong. After ten years the drug had taken all that he had and all that he was. Living as a crackhead was not the life he wants. Death appears to be the better option.

He is about to climb back on the ledge when he hears, "I wish all y'all would die. Y'all take so much from everybody dat knows ya. One crackhead can destroy a whole family. Da shit spreads. One mothafucker come home smokin' dat shit, da next thing ya know da whole damn family smokin', sellin' or something. Da shit is a disease, a plague. It's evil. So jump, boy, and do yaself and da people dat loves ya a favor. Go on, finish ya high!"

Deacon pauses, "Did your crackhead jump from here wino? Did you watch her? Did you try to stop her?"

"Shut up! Just shut ya damn mouth."

"Was she one of the two that jumped last week?"

"Ain't cha got somethin' to do crack-head?"

"Was she?"

"No!"

"Is she dead?"

"Yeah, she's dead. She died here, but not last week. She died over a month ago. She was in misery, just like all of y'all. She tried to stop a hundred times, but couldn't. She came from nowhere. I found her up here, just like a stray pup. She was curled up on dis roof, cold, wet and cryin'. I watched befo' I said anythang to her. She didn't see me.

"Den after awhile, when I saw she wasn't movin, I walked over to her. She was out of her mind wid fever. I took her to my room. I fed her, bathed her and let her rest. She slept fo' a week.

"It was like ya said, she was good company. I knew what she was. When she got her health back, she went back to gettin' high. She'd go off for a day or so and come back tired and dirty, just like a stray. She'd cry and pray and promise herself, not me, herself, she wouldn't do it again. But she did.

"Den she disappeared fo' two weeks. I heard about da first girl dat jumped from here. I thought it was her. It wasn't. I started comin' up here every night cause I knew she'd come back here. I seen three of y'all crack-heads come up here and jump.

"Da first one I tried to stop. He looked me straight in da eye befo' he jumped. Misery was all I saw in his eyes. Da second one I grabbed and begged not to jump; but soon as I let her go, she dived over da ledge. Da third one, I didn't say or do nothin', I just watched. I figured da first one picked dis buildin' because it was the only five story buildin' around. Da other two I guess they came up because it was monkey see, monkey do.

"It's sad, but I guess it's a endin' to it. She stopped here. Da night I found her she worse dan befo'. She couldn't even stand. She'd been beaten. I picked her up so easy it scared me. She had no weight. She was nothin' but bones. In her eyes I saw nothin' but misery. I carried her over to the ledge and let her go.

"Nobody came to my room askin' bout her. No family, no police, nobody came, nobody cared. It was over fo' her. I stayed in my room for a month. Last week I came back up here to sit and drank and the first thing I saw was another one of y'all sittin' on dat ledge cryin'. I walked behind him and pushed him over. Ended it fo' him too. Den it was the girl that was just sittin' there cryin' and smoking that mess at the same time. I pushed her over too.

"Dis was always a good place to sit and drank, but y'all crack-heads . . . y'all added da show. And tonight boy, you da star. So, go on back out dere on dat ledge. And finish ya high."

"Damn, you're a sick motherfucker! You can't simply kill people!"

"Y'all ain't people! Y'all is crack-heads! Ya know ya ain't shit. And ya know ya ain' gonna get no better. Endin' it's da only way. Y'all's a cancer dats got to be cut out befo' ya destroy everybody. Ya know ya cain't change. Ain't no hope fo' ya boy. Don't lie to yaself crack-head. Go on back on dat ledge boy and finish ya high."

"If you wanted to see me die, why did you stop me? Why didn't you just let me jump?"

"Just fuckin wid cha. I was just addin' a little spice. You can go on and jump now."

Cautiously Deacon steps away from the ledge, "I am a real person, not a stray animal or cancer. Crack-heads are people. We have a disease; we are not the disease. I can change."

"Bullshit boy! A zebra cain't change its stripes, boy."

"I am not an animal! I am a human being."

"You a crackhead."

"Fuck you, man. I'm not jumping."

"What?"

"I'm not jumping."

"Ya gotta jump. Death is callin'."

"No man. I am not doing it. I got a choice. I can change."

"You as miserable as da others dat came up here. Dat kind of misery don't go away boy. I know. Ain't no hope fo' ya crackhead. Ya know ya tried to stop befo' and ya couldn't. How many times? How many lies? How many lives of other folks have ya messed up? You are da disease crack-head. Do ya part and stop spreadin' it. Death is callin' boy. Finish ya high crack-head. Goddamit jump!"

"Look a here you crazy motherfucker. I'm not jumping!"

"Get ya miserable crackhead ass back on dat ledge and jump!"

"No!"

"Jump!"

"Fuck you!" Deacon spins around and flees through the door and down the ragged steps. He doesn't slow down until he hits street level.

"That crazy motherfucker was trying to kill me!" He says out loud to those passing by, but no one stops to listen. He looks up to the top of the building and sees the old wino standing on the ledge. He watches a bottle fall from the wino's hand. He sees it shatter on the pavement about ten feet away from him. He sees the wino step from the ledge into the night air. He sees his body land without splatter, in the middle of the avenue.

"Damn!"

3

A Brother's Death

The red brick edges of the building's corner dug through his green nylon jacket into his shoulder. Despite the pain he stayed against the laundromat's wall and slithered into the alley. They needed to stay in the shadows the darkness was the only cover available. Freddy tried to stay there, but he stumbled into the streetlight and Satan's Posse's bullets were quick to put him to rest. No, he and his brother were not to going make that mistake. Three blocks, if they remained cloaked in the shadows and moved quickly, they could reach the safety of their own hood.

He heard his brother's long breaths; he was keeping up. His brother caught a Satan's Posse bullet in the thigh during the robbery. The stickup was Freddy's idea. It sounded stupid, but he thought being broke was dumber. So, he convinced his younger brother to go along with them to rob the largest crack-house Satan's Posse ran.

With a bag of money in one hand and a pistol in the other, climbing the junkyard fence at the end of the alley was not an option. He chose to go back to the shadows of the blocks. He made a u-turn threw himself against the other wall and headed for the alley's opening.

A way to safety appeared at the mouth of the alley. A cab pulled up and the driver hung out the window regurgitating. A quick jack and they would be home free. Steps away from the cab he heard a low voice call, "Richard!" It was the panic whisper of his younger brother. He stopped for the first time since robbing the crack-house.

"Richard!" He turned and saw his brother had tried to climb the fence and was stuck, laying prone across the top horizontal pole. He looked back to the cab. The cabby wouldn't be tossin' his cookies long was his thought. The plan to hi-jack the cabby was aborted by his brother's plea.

"They gonna see me, Richard. Come, get me down!!!"

"Damn it!" He spun around and returned to the fence. His brother's belt buckle and shoelace were caught in the top links. He was wound too tight to stand still in front of the fence. He paced the fence. He never allowed robbery loot leave his hands. Putting down the money and his pistol, didn't feel right to him, but he didn't have a choice. Midway up the fence he was able to unhook his brother who landed on the other side.

"Climb back over before the dogs come!"

"Ain't no dogs, you come this way."

They spoke through the darkness. "You wrong, boy, ain't nothin' but hell hounds over here!"

He heard the popping of the pistols. He dived to the ground for his gun. His brother's body laid before him on the other side of the fence, blocking bullets. He wanted to stand and empty his chamber, but that would not have been street smart. He grabbed the loot and crawled away from the alley.

4

My Father's Day

Do I hate my father? No not really. It wasn't done out of hate. It was done out of ability. Why he called after fifteen years is still unknown to me. Ok, I understand he is dying and trying to get things right in his life, but what was a visit supposed to do. What did he think would be accomplished? The man's health is not a concern of mine; how could he think it would. He left my mother and me fifteen years ago. Left us, broke. The man didn't send one dime over fifteen years, and now a phone call.

Hostility is a negative emotion that takes its physical toll on the carrier. At least that's what I read in a health magazine about ulcers. I was very hostile towards my father, but not anymore. We will never be friends or anything; but the hatred that was there has lessened. Most people may feel guilty or regretful after such an act, not me. The act was good for several concerns, and more than I benefited from the deed.

My mother told me my father left because he fell in love with another woman. When I was eight years old, she told me that men often find other women to be in love with and leave their wives and family. I remember not wanting to be a man, not wanting to do something as hurtful as my father had done.

My mother cried for a lot of nights after he left. We cried for a lot of nights after he left. Mama told me to stop crying because I had to be the man of the house. I didn't want to be the man of the house. I didn't want to stop crying. I wanted my daddy back, but he didn't come back, he didn't call and, according my mother, he just didn't give a damn about us.

Mama stopped crying over him and told me to stop crying over him too. When she caught me crying, after she decided it was time for us to stop crying, I got a beating with the extension cord. I soon stopped crying about daddy too.

After mama stopped crying, it didn't take her long to move in "step-daddies and uncles"—three step daddies and two uncles to be exact. We found out that step-daddies and uncles leave families too. Only mothers stayed.

Last week a local cable station interviewed me. The Athens Voice, my alternative weekly paper, has been winning awards; one for fiction, one for the best alternative weekly and one for best investigative reporting for an alternative weekly. It was all due to my staff not me. I was fortunate enough to have passionate people work at The Athens Voice from day one. My father saw the interview, got a contact number from the show and called me.

My initial response was "Hell no"! However, the reporter's curiosity in me got the best of past pains and disappointments. My father's address was one of wealth; only very rich people resided in that section of the city. I was aware of the fact that no Blacks were living there; only white Anglo Saxon Protestants lived in the area.

I went to see my father, hoping he was the dying butler of some rich white folks. I went to laugh in his dying face. I carried around a lot of hate for a twenty-three year old. My doctor told me I was his youngest patient with ulcers.

There was no butler at the address. My father lived in a coach-house of one of the estates. His woman, his white woman was the niece of the owners. The rented the coach-house to her. He lived with her. For some reason I remembered my father as a much darker man and a taller man. I am at least half a foot taller and my pecan brown skin was three shades lighter than his blonde oak colored skin. He actually smiled, no grinned happily when he saw me.

He was sitting on a couch wrapped in multi-colored striped blanket. The sun was shinning brightly through the small paned windows behind him. Looking at him wrapped in a blanket,

I thought about the cold nights we had in the little house he left us in that first winter. We couldn't pay the gas bill and the electric heater didn't stay on long either. We moved from the house to the projects. I moved Mama out of the projects four months ago, bought her a nice ranch home. I paid for it in full. I have a mortgage on my condo, but Mama's home is paid for.

I smiled back at him, actually sat next to him on the couch and hugged him. I didn't become a youngest alternative newspaper publisher in the city without learning how to play games. I can smile on the outside and frown on the inside with the best of them.

We had about fifteen minutes of slightly difficult small talk. It was a little awkward for him to talk around abandoning us, but he did it up until his white woman said lunch was ready. It was troublesome for him to move from the couch, so I helped her bring in trays. I also helped her carry in food from the grill on the porch.

It was lovely back yard, manicured lawn and a landscaped flower garden. My father's white woman loved flowers. She said her uncle had the landscaping done for her. We had a good conversation out by the grill. She was actually closer to me in age than to my father. Last week she graduated from grad school with her MBA and was on her way to California.

She'd met my father two years ago; he sold hotdogs from a cart on her campus. One thing led to another, good conversations at the cart, led to going out for coffee, then dates. He spent the night, one night and never left. He wasn't sick then at least not to her knowledge. He became sick five months ago, liver and prostate cancer. He wasn't expected to make through the year.

Her eyes watered when she said that. I gave her what I thought would be a consoling hug; however, our bodies clung to each other a little longer than I intended. We were still in an embrace when she said she wasn't sure of what to do with my father. Theirs was not to be a long-term relationship.

When she broke the embrace, she said he'd asked to go to California with her, but that was completely out of the question and she wasn't sure how to tell him. She said it was a godsend that they were watching the cable station and saw me. Her hopes were that I would assist in finding him a home.

It appeared my father had no idea he was about to be homeless. His white woman had a one-way ticket for a flight to California in two weeks. I initiated a tight embrace and told her she had nothing to worry about, of course I would find my father shelter. The embrace ended with my patting her quite heavy handedly on her plump little behind. She giggled and I smiled.

During lunch it became apparent that my father hadn't told his white woman about how he left my mother and me. The story was that they divorced amicably and he assisted in paying for my college education. I never went to college. I graduated high school from night school. And if Nicholas, my business backer and lover, had not been so set on education, I wouldn't have gotten that. I was selling ads for another alternative weekly and making a ton of money from the time I was sixteen years old. I never valued education.

I managed to nod to my head affirmatively through most of the lies that were spewed through lunch. I was able to do this because I really didn't hear half of what was said because my mind was calculating my father's painful demise. Sitting next to him on the couch, I actually saw how thin and weak he actually was. I was sure he had become a burden to his white woman. I was about to comment on that when he asked how my mother was doing as if he had seen her last week.

I told him she was doing fine in her new home and had recently returned from Jamaica. I told him her health was good. Then, I lied and said she runs three miles a day since mobility was an obvious problem for him. Whenever I felt him looking at me, I placed my eyes intently in his white woman's crotch. She was wearing shorts that displayed her camel toes. I hadn't slept with a woman in over two years, but doing the deed wasn't problem for me. Since I had never slept with a white woman, I was actually a little excited by the prospect.

I figured having a sick prostate had limited his performance in the sexual arena. Because of the way his white woman giggled from the pat on the butt I gave her, it was obvious she was a little needy in that area. He noticed my eyes on her camel toes. She smiled, he cleared his throat and asked when was I leaving. I told him I was thinking about making a day out of it since it had been so long since we talked. I gathered his dishes and mine and walked to the kitchen. His white woman followed me with her dishes in hand. As soon as she entered the kitchen, I grabbed a hold of her and kissed hard and rugged. She returned every bit of tongue and pressure.

She felt my erection and began grinding on it. When I was fully stretched out, I stopped her and walked back to the front area for my father to see. His eyes went straight to my lump. I sat down right next to him. His white woman didn't follow me; she went to their bedroom. He tried to stand and fell back down to the couch. I stood and offered him a hand, he refused and tried to stand again, he failed again. He took my hand for his third attempt and rose. He took one feeble step and tripped over my outstretched foot. I offered my assistance again, but he crawled back to the couch and climbed up it. He said what I was doing wasn't right. I laughed hard in his face.

I pulled out my cell phone and dialed the county hospital. He heard me telling the operator that I had a homeless cancer patient that needed hospitalization. When he heard me give her his name, he started having a coughing spell. I patted him hard on the back. Spittle cleared his throat and he thanked me.

When his white woman joined us again, she had on a housecoat and I heard him moan. She sat in the chair across from us. I stood up and went and stood behind her chair. I called him Dad when I told him that his white woman was leaving for California and she wouldn't be able to take him. Furthermore, we decided that his housing should be left in my hands. My hands were on her shoulders as I spoke. He lowered his head. His white woman said something about the water spout on tub being stuck and asked could I check it for her.

The noises we made from the bedroom must have made him try again to get up. We heard the thud. When we got into the living area, he was laying prone on the floor. He didn't come to until the ambulance came to transport him to the county hospital.

My mother has gone to see him twice; she said it is the Christian thing to do. I have never gone to see him and don't plan to. She maintained a life insurance policy on him and claims that it will be enough to bury him proper. If I have my way, he will get cremated and I'll be on my way to the Lexus dealership. The cremation wouldn't be out of hate because I don't hate my father, but I do love a Lexus. I am a man who believes a person should use their abilities to get what they want. Why my father called me, I don't know. I do know I had the ability to relieve myself of fifteen years of hostility and I did just that.

5

Time to Go

It was the one of the largest phone rooms in the city and the only one on the South Side. The company employed mostly Blacks as telemarketers. A lot families on the South Side depended on this room. Single mothers who worked part-time and went to school, college and high school students, even grown people who couldn't get work elsewhere, could go in there and pick up a phone for four hours a day and get paid. It wasn't good pay, but it was pay. No one bragged about working there but for the four years the room was there, people were grateful to have an employer on their side of the city.

The building the phone room was housed in was originally built to be a grocery store. Fifteen years ago it was "The Corner Family Store" until old man D'Mantio died. Since none of his children wanted to run a store, Amir and his brothers took it over until they brought a bigger store on the avenue.

Ten years ago Pastor Sellaman and his church brought the building and held services in it for a good while, then the pastor died. After that the building stayed empty for a year or so before Murray Telephone Sales Company took it over.

They turned the grocery building into an office building. People new to the area, like Fred Sikes, had no idea the phone room they worked in was once a grocery store. The Murray Telephone Sales Company did a good job in converting the corner store building into an office building. They did better than Pastor Sellaman's flock; all the church folks did was haul out all the shelves and put in some chairs.

The Murray Telephone Sales Company gutted the place and built new walls and added a new beige and gray stone tile floor, they even redid the bird-cage office that was above the store in the back.

When any person first walked into the phone room, he or she was greeted by a smiling Mrs. Millie Murray, the owner's wife. She may be the only person in the city still wearing her silver blue hair in a beehive hair style. It has been said that Mrs. Millie's porcelain tea cup holds more than tea. Her continuous sipping throughout the morning causes her to be unable to work the afternoon. However, most mornings she greets those that enter the phone room with a warm cheerful greeting and peppermint scented smile.

Behind Mrs. Millie desk are five rows of chest high office cubicles, each cubicle held one rep. Above the white and tan office cubicles were hanging spot lights, they light the room well, every letter and number on a reps key board can be seen.

All the computer monitors were flat screens which gave the room a high-tech feel. The flat screens and the computer dialing systems came with Mr. Murray's son, Marcus Jr. who had recently graduated from college and joined his father's sales company. Due to Marcus's obesity and premature balding; the family resemblance between he and the tall, slender, well groomed and impeccable dressed Mr. Murray went unnoticed.

The conversational buzz one heard, when entering the phone room, was strong because folks that worked there were always "dialing for dollars" as Mr. Murray was fond of saying. A full room was thirty reps and the room was always full. The company operated on four-hour shifts, six days a week beginning at seven Monday morning and ending at eleven Saturday night. An employee was hired part-time to work one shift a day, but the company would allow a rep that had made quota to stay for another shift.

A rep that was making quota could have worked as many shifts as desired. The rep that was not making quota was sent home after the second hour of their four-hour shift. The policy of sending non-productive reps home, also came with Mr. Murray's son, Junior.

The new policy had been discussed between management and the employees two months prior to it actually being enforced. The employees didn't think it would come to pass because Mr. Murray had always let them work their four-hour shift, despite quota. It was common knowledge that as an employee you were guaranteed at least the four hours. No one had ever worked less than a four-hour shift.

Marcus Jr. changed what was common knowledge and began sending reps home after two hours. The first week the policy was in place every rep who was sent home went up to the bird-cage to talk to Mr. Murray, thinking it would make difference. Each rep came down from the cage disappointed. Mr. Murray shook his styled gray-ish blond hair to the negative, telling each rep that Junior ran the floor and whatever his decisions were; they were final. Marcus gave each complaining rep a smile and a nod as they left the phone room, along with a 'better luck tomorrow' wave.

During the second week with Junior's policy in place, the reps began to argue over seating assignments, believing that certain terminals produced better leads. Jr. handled the problem by sending the reps home who wouldn't sit in assigned seats.

Junior installed a row of ten seats in the back of the phone room. In those seats sat reps waiting to work extra hours. If a rep working his or her normal shift and didn't make quota in two hours, a waiting rep who had made quota from another shift, was given the seat. In the weeks that followed the pay that wasn't good pay from the start became less for a lot of reps. For those that could sell using Junior's program, it was a godsend and they made more money than ever. Fred Sikes, a former supervisor who was demoted along with the other five supervisors, was among those who made less under Junior's new plan.

After Marcus Jr. installed the automated dialing system, he told his father the need for floor supervisors had diminished. The computers tallied calls and kept a history of each reps performance, what he needed he told his father, were mangers educated managers who would be concerned about cost and profits. He convinced his father that two managers would be more profitable in the long run than six supervisors. And as luck would have it, two of his fraternity brothers, both with degrees in Business Management were available.

Mr. Murray had not been completely in favor of the idea of getting rid of the supervisors. He had promoted each one of them from reps to supervisors, they were his team. For four years following his directives; they kept the business in the black. But the numbers Junior brought back did impress him. The kid hadn't been wrong yet. As a compromise he asked Junior could at least one of the supervisors, Fred Sikes, be a manager. Junior flat out refused. He wanted the managers to be degreed. Mr. Murray gave Junior his way and his team of supervisors was replaced with Junior's two managers.

Mr. Murray, an old 'tin man' who was forced out of home remodeling business by the district attorney's office, never saw himself as a business man. He liked to think of himself as a salesman, nothing more. He enjoyed going out and bringing in new business. Before Junior his team of supervisors pretty much ran the day-to-day business of the company. From the steady stream of telemarketers that came through his front door he was able to find a bookkeeper, a personnel person and a general manager and they all got the same title of "Supervisor". They were happy to be promoted from the phones and he was happy not to have to pay them the amount that their duties truly were worth.

Fred Sikes, the General Manager Supervisor, was the only one he paid close to what he was worth. He knew the severe cut in pay had to be dramatic for him. He'd expected Fred to come up to the bird-cage last week when Junior first sent him home, but Fred left without a word. This was unusual because Fred was definitely the squeaky wheel of all his supervisors. Whenever he viewed something as unfair, Fred would launch a complaint. His silence had worried Mr. Murray. But what worried him more that last day, was watching Jr. laughing in Fred's face when he tapped him on the shoulder to let him know that he was under quota and had to give up his seat.

"Looks like you're short, Fred." Junior spoke loudly so that the whole room could hear him, "Up the seat baby! Better luck tomorrow."

Fred felt Junior's hand on the back of his chair, shaking it and he heard him snickering. Junior thought sending a man home from work early was funny. Junior thought cutting a grown man's pay who had a wife to support was funny. Junior thought sending a guy back to the phones after he had already paid his dues on the phones was funny. In Fred's opinion, Junior thought a lot of sick shit was funny.

"You know what, Junior. I don't think I'm leaving today." Fred hadn't raised his voice. He spoke only for Junior to hear.

"That's Mr. Murray on the floor." Junior bellowed. "Don't let me have to tell you that again Fred. And what do you mean, you don't think you're leaving. You're short; you go. And bro you're short!"

"I need to talk to Mr. Murray."

Fred wasn't sure what was going on with the company, but he had come to end of his patience. Whatever Mr. Murray was planning, Fred felt it was past time that he included him in on it. He sat patiently the first month because he had enough overrides and past commissions to carry him. His check didn't drop much until last payday. Last payday he earned what a rep earned and his responsibilities had grown past a rep's pay.

He didn't leave the company like the other supervisors because he was certain that Mr. Murray had a plan for him. He just hadn't told him yet. Once he met with him and told him how tight things had become financially, he was certain Mr. Murray would include him on what was happening.

Fred tried to convince the other supervisors to stay and wait out whatever was happening. He was unsuccessful; the two women had new jobs one week after Junior brought in the two managers. They told the men they had better find something while Mr. Murray was still given the references. That made sense to the other men and by the end of the first month they had new jobs as well. Fred thought they were all being disloyal. How could they abandon a man that had given them a chance? Fred wasn't going to run like a coward. He was certain Mr. Murray had a plan; he just had to be patient. But with Jr. shaking his chair, with his pay way too short and him the last remaining supervisor, he felt it was time he talked to Mr. Murray.

"I'm going up to the bird-cage to see Mr. Murray. Do you want to try to climb the stairs with me?" Fred being of short slender stature was able to stand up quickly from the chair.

It was common knowledge within the room that the stairs were a challenge to Junior. His obesity kept him from climbing them regularly. There were thirty-two stairs up to the bird-cage. Junior would almost die after eight.

"My dad doesn't want to be bothered by reps today." Junior grabbed a hold of Fred's shoulder. "I suggest you leave."

Fred spun around and placed both his open palms against Junior's chest and shoved. The force of Fred's push, along with Junior's weight and gravity, had Junior toddling across the room. If the wall had been half a step away, Junior would have fallen to the floor.

"Both of you guys get up here now!" Mr. Murray yelled from the bird-cage, he'd been watching them from above the room.

In his heart Mr. Murray knew it would come to this. Fred was a good kid, a hard worker who expected to be treated fairly. Marcus Jr. up until now had never amounted to anything. If it wasn't for his wife's constant nagging, Mr. Murray wouldn't have put Junior in charge of the coffee pot, never mind the day-to-day operations of the company. Mrs. Murray convinced him by making the point that trusting in Junior to run the company would build his character. Mr. Murray felt four years of college should have built the boys character.

In the past anything that required Junior to work, he didn't do. The boy was just lazy, through and through and Mr. Murray didn't think allowing him to run the company would change that, but he turned out to be wrong. Millie was right, once he showed faith in his son, the boy came through. Junior proved himself with the recent sales numbers and the plain simple truth was, that for once, Mr. Murray was proud of his fat son.

Fred made it through the office door first. Mr. Murray heard the stairs creaking from the weight of his son climbing them. He wasn't far behind Fred, who entered the office steaming angry. Fred was thinking how dare Junior put his hands on him and it was time for some answers.

He stood in front of Mr. Murray's desk and said, "What's going on Boss? Things are getting crazy around here. How long are you going to let Junior treat people like this? I really need to know what's going on and when I can expect my pay to return to normal and how much longer are we going to have to put up Junior running the floor?"

"Fred, I'm going to have to let you go." Mr. Murray said with a straight face. There was no sign of humor; he looked serious to Fred.

"What?"

"I can't have you putting your hands on my son. Clear your desk. I'll mail you your check. That's all, Fred."

"I'm fired?" Fred took a step beck from the desk, a little disorientated. Anger gave way to disappointment.

Junior and one other manager had made it up the stairs and into the office. They were standing behind Fred.

"Yes, but I'll take care of you. We will pay you out at the supervisor's rate. See to it Marcus."

"Dad, I don't see why we should do that his current status is rep." Junior objected.

"Yes well, I want you to pay him out as a supervisor. Understand!"

"I'm fired?" Fred said again.

The question went unanswered. No one said a word, but the manager and Junior snickered.

"Boss, we can work something out."

"There is nothing to work out, Fred. You can't push my son. He's your boss. I'll tell you what; I'm going to cut you check right now for a grand. If we owe you more, Marcus will send it to you."

Mr. Murray pulled out his check book and wrote the thousand dollar check.

"Dad, we don't owe him any where close to that amount!"

Mr. Murray handed the check to Fred. He took the check while trying to look his ex-boss in the eye. Mr. Murray would not look at him eye-to-eye.

"I worked here for four years, Boss. I was the second person you hired when you open the doors. I didn't think I was going to get job because I had never sold anything before. You told me, if I could sell myself to you in the interview; I could sell on the phone. I had a lot of jobs, but I had never been promoted on any of them. You made me a supervisor, Boss; that meant something to me. . ."

"Fred, this is business and all business relationships end."

"Come to think about it, Boss I have never been fired before either: you the only person that promoted me and fired me."

From Junior came, "All that's very touching Fred. You got the check, now get your stuff and leave."

Fred was the last remaining part of the old system—his Dad's system. Junior wanted the room to be his, all his. He wanted it to reflect how he thought a sales company should run. He envisioned an environment driven by profit. He didn't want reps loyal to him. He wanted them loyal to their own gain, thereby, being loyal to profit. Fred was loyal to his father, not profit. In Junior's opinion Fred was a lack-luster sales guy that his father liked. He had no room for people like him in the company he envisioned.

"You know what Junior. Fuck you, man awright! I'm leaving, but not because you breathing all down my back and shit. You don't scare me with your fat ass! Matter of fact" Fred spun around fast and said; "Fuck all y'all!"

He walked out The Murray Telephone Sales Company without looking back. He wanted to look back, but he didn't want anyone to see the tears that had welled up in his eyes. "All business relationships end", Mr. Murray's words repeatedly ran through his mind—all business relationships end, all business relationships end, all business relationships end. "But I thought we was friends Boss." Fred kept his head down as he walked the five blocks to his apartment.

He didn't notice that it was a sunny day. He didn't notice the buds on the tree branches were ready to open, nor did he notice the rich green of the new grass. What he did notice was a broken wine bottle, an empty crack bag and two dogs mating behind a metal fence. Apartment buildings filled the blocks of his neighborhood with an occasional house stuck in between the larger apartment buildings. The humping dogs were behind the fence of a house. His building was two blocks down.

It was cool being able to walk to work. It never took him more than fifteen minutes to make it there, even in the snow or rain. He was a block away from home when he stopped walking. A thousand dollars could carry him for a couple of weeks, but he had to find a job. He just got fired. The library was two blocks to the left up on the avenue. He decided to go there and look through that day and Sunday's paper.

He had to walk past Amir and his brother's liquor store before he got to the library. The thought of drinking a pint of wine came strong into his mind, but he walked past the store and into the library next door. Today's paper along with Sunday's paper was already on the front counter. He took both to a table and sat down with them.

Between the two papers he found eight jobs that he qualified for, three were entry-level management positions. He smiled when he looked down at the list he compiled, "Damn a brother is kind of qualified to some things" he said to himself.

He used the small pieces of scrap paper and the short pencils that were on top of the card catalog cases to write down the jobs. He had eight scraps of paper with a perspective job on each. All the companies were either downtown or on the north side. The ten minute short walks to work would be over. Another thing that made him smile was that all the jobs he intended on applying for paid more than what Mr. Murray paid him.

He put the newspapers back on the counter and slid the scrap paper notes into his wallet. He dropped the short pencil back in the little cardboard box and headed home. Since he had a plan of action, he felt better about going home and telling his wife about getting fired. When they got married, he didn't have a job and neither did she. Over the past four years they both have become employed and secured a nice apartment with some nice things, including six year old Volvo which his wife used to get to work.

When Fred entered the apartment, he heard his wife in the bedroom humming; she was getting ready for work. He entered the bedroom and smiled at her cherry colored Certified Nurse's

Aide uniform. She finished the training program to be a Certified Nurse's Aide six months prior; she had a permanent position for three weeks only.

"Oh, you're home Freddy, good+. You can drive me to work, and then, get the oil in the car changed. I didn't have time to do it this morning; I don't know where the time went."

Just seeing her took the little bit of the remaining sadness away. He always felt lucky to have her as a wife. Her round pretty face, well rounded hips and thick hair warmed his heart on sight. She'd married him when he had nothing, because she said she loved him and believed everything else would work out.

"Baby, I got something to tell you."

"Tell me in the car, I got to go." She slid into her white easy walking shoes and made it to the front door. He stood in the bedroom.

"Are you coming?" She called from the open door.

"Right behind you Baby."

In the car, as he pulled away from the curb he said, "Baby, I got fired today." He looked over to Tammy quickly. She really hadn't heard him; she was putting on her eyeliner.

"What did you say, Freddy?"

"I sort of got fired today." He looked at her and saw that she stopped putting on the eyeliner.

"How do you 'sort of get fired'.? Were you laid off?"

"No, Baby, I wasn't laid off."

"Then, you were fired."

"Yeah, Baby, I was fired."

"Why? What happened? What did you do?"

Fred stopped at a stop sign. He didn't want to answer why, what happened or what did he do.

"I really didn't do anything, Baby."

He was going the wrong way for her job, but she didn't notice. He turned the corner and went around the block and headed in the right direction.

"Come on, Freddy, tell me what happened. I deserve to know the truth."

She didn't sound mad; she sounded more concerned than anything else.

"It just wasn't working out anymore, Baby. I tried but it wasn't working out."

Tammy turned around in the car seat so she could face him. "What wasn't working out? What do you mean you tried? You have to tell me more than that, Freddy."

"OK, do you remember when I told you about Junior sending me home last week?"

"Yeah."

"Well, that was just start. Today he was yelling at me on the floor, totally disrespecting me."

"But I thought you and Junior were working together?"

"Not after he phased out the supervisors. I swear, Baby, it felt like he was after me. He was always looking over my shoulder, checking and double-checking my orders, just bugging me. Sending me home last week was just the start, the writing was on the wall."

"So Junior fired you?"

"No, his father did."

"Mr. Murray fired you? Freddy that's hard to believe; he liked you so much. What did he say?"

"The man told me all business relationships come to an end and that we were at the end of ours. He said it was only business."

"Shut up!" She said honestly shocked.

"That's what the man said."

"So, what made him fire you; he had to have a specific reason?" Looking out the passenger window Tammy said, "Freddy, you just missed the turn for my job."

"My bad, Baby." He made a U-turn on the street.

"So, tell me what happened."

"Look I may be short on some of the details, but I pretty much told you what happened."

"No, you haven't. All you told me was you got fired—not why. I am not a child, Freddy. Don't play with me. Now tell me what happened."

Now, he heard the anger in her voice he had expected.

"Freddy, we need that job."

"I know that, Tammy."

"We can't afford for you to get fired. There must be something you can do to get the job back. Maybe tomorrow you can go back and talk to Mr. Murray."

"What! Talk about what, Baby? He and I just got through talking."

"Freddy, there must be something you can say or do to get the job back! You've been there for four years! People don't get fired after four years."

"Well, Baby, I did."

"Freddy, you are going the wrong damn way to my job! What are you trying to get me fired too?"

Fred pulled the car over and stopped in front of the library.

"I can't drive there, Baby, my head is all messed up. You mind if I get out and walk home from here. We can talk tonight."

"Fine, Freddy."

She jumped out and went around to the driver's side before he could get the door open. He tried to kiss her on the cheek once she was in the driver's seat; but she moved out of his reach.

"See you tonight" she said, pulling into the street. He waved good bye. She didn't.

Fred Sikes didn't hesitate one minute. He walked straight into the liquor store and brought a fifth of blended whiskey. When he got home, he didn't bother with cup or ice, nor did he take the fifth bottle out of the brown paper bag. He sat at the table and turned it up time and time again. At twenty-eight he wasn't a much better a drinker than he was in high school. Liquid courage is what his daddy called liquor.

"Somebody should go up there and teach his fat ass a lesson . . . - treating people like shit. Somebody's going to show them one day. Black people don't take shit like that. One day somebody going to get they white asses straight. When Boss had us supervising, it was all right, but it's not all right with all white people in charge. The brothers ain't going to stand for that. They're going to want to see a Black manager.

"Damn! . . . I should go up there and tell Boss that. I bet he didn't even think about that. He got to have at least one Black in management. Shit, it might as well be me. Let me go put on my suit, so he can see I got one and that I can dress just as good as the other managers."

While attempting to tie his tie, the thought entered his mind that he should take his pistol up to The Murray Telephones Sales Company. In case Mr. Murray said no to his good idea, at least he could have some fun by scaring the shit out of Junior.

Of course he planned on the emptying the gun of its shells, but when he looked at the dresser clock and saw that shift change was less than a half an hour away, he got in a hurry He remembered to grab the pistol, but forgot to take out the shells.

Mrs. Murray, who at that time of day was almost as tipsy as Fred, forgot about him being fired earlier and waved him past her. Junior's back was turned as he walked right passed him and up to the bird-cage. Mr. Murray saw him coming and wondered why he was dressed in a suit. He called down to Junior and told him to come up to the cage with the other manager.

As soon as Fred walked into the office, Mr. Murray smelled the liquor. The kid had gone and got drunk, Mr. Murray thought he would have done the same thing.

"Boss, I thought about something and I had to tell you." Fred stood swaying in front of the desk.

"What's that Fred?" Mr. Murray remained seated, it was easier to reach the pistol from the bottom drawer if he needed it, but he didn't think he would need it.

"You don't have any Black managers, but you have all Blacks on the phones. You need a Black manager, Boss."

"We never hired by race in the past. What makes you think we would start now."

"Never hired buy race in the past? Boss, you got all Black people working for you. You had to hire by race."

"No, Fred, it just worked out that way because this was the only area where I could afford to buy the space that I needed. I didn't set out to hire all Blacks."

"Well, that's what you got! And you are going to need a Black manager, especially with Junior ruffling folks' feathers like he's doing. Black people don't like taking that much shit from white people."

Looking past Fred down onto the floor, Mr. Murray saw Junior and the manager involved in another confrontation with a rep. No, it looked like there were two or three reps arguing with Junior and the manager while Mrs. Murray was staggering towards the yelling crowd.

"Hold on a second, Fred. There is a problem downstairs."

Mr. Murray was up and down the stairs before Fred actually understood what he said. Fred stood up and looked out the office window to the floor and said, "Told you."

The whole room was in an uproar. Reps, who were to be sent home; were refusing to go. Fred heard them screaming that they were hired to work four hours, not two. A crowd of fifteen or more reps was backing Mr. Murray, Mrs. Murray, Jr. and the manager against the back wall. The ten reps who had made quota and where waiting for a seat: got up and fled when the crowd continued to advance to the back.

The screams were no longer about being wronged for hours, Fred heard people yelling things like, "Let's beat they white asses."

"Shit, Boss needs my help!"

Fred drew his pistol and stumbled down the stairs more than he ran down them. When got downstairs, five people already had Junior on the ground kicking him good.

"Hey!" Fred shouted, "I got a gun!"

No one responded, they continued to stomp Junior and more had surrounded his manager. The manager's fatal mistake was saying, "You stupid niggers better get away from me."

The crowd swarmed him. Fred was pushing Mr. and Mrs. Murray up to the front with the gun in his hand when the police came through the front door. They saw the gun and him pushing two elderly looking white people. They shot Fred twenty-six times.

The Murray Telephone Sales Company and the corner it sat on was the focal point of that evening's news. One television station refereed to it as a 'race incident' with one white man, a manager, being beaten to death. Another station focused on the angry employees and their violated rights as the cause of 'the incident on the South Side'.

Junior was interviewed, swollen and bruised from his hospital bed. He was quoted saying that he was only trying to make things better and give people an opportunity to make more money. When asked would the company reopen its doors, he said not in the same location.

The television station that kept the highest ratings was the one that reported the story between Mr. Murray and his former employee Fred Sikes. Fred Sikes was who accidentally shot twenty-six times by the police had Type O negative blood. In order to save his life, the paramedics needed to do an immediate blood transfusion. The person who was on the scene with Type O negative blood was his former employer Mr. Murray. Mr. Murray volunteered to be the blood donor.

Fred Sikes, whose wife was expecting their first child at the time of the shooting, recovered and his attorney was successful in securing a settlement large enough to allow Fred to purchase the property from Mr. Murray and open the Sikes Telephone Sales Company (STSC). STSC became the number one telephone sales company in the city.

6

A Memorable Elevator Ride

D o you mind if I bend your ear for a moment? The strangest thing just happened to me and I must tell someone. Do you have a minute? You're not going to believe this. Did you know my office is on the thirty-six floor? Well, it is. The elevators are always breaking down, so I wasn't surprised to see two service people on the elevator. I was going to pass on the car until the worker holding a ladder waved me in.

While standing facing the door, I heard one of them say, "Good afternoon".

I assumed one service worker was speaking to the other, I didn't answer. My mind was racing with meeting plans. I heard the second greeting, but I didn't consider it. Again I was preoccupied with the meeting plans. It wasn't until one of the service workers rudely pushed past me to get to the control panel did I began to notice things.

The worker opened the panel and flipped the biggest switch behind it. The car jerked to a stop. I was startled, but not afraid. A service worker stopped the elevator; a service worker could start the elevator. I stood calmly for a minute or so until I noticed neither worker was working on elevator.

I looked at both of them and saw that they were Black men. The one who opened the panel looked a little like Kenny Jameson, a high-school classmate of mine, who is now serving time for rape, or so I heard. The service worker returned to the panel box flipped another switch and the lights went out.

All I had for a weapon was my fountain pen. I was stabbing into the darkness with it when the lights flipped back on. I tried to act as if I hadn't moved because I saw neither one of them had moved. However, they where both laughing at me; they saw my defensive actions with the ink pen.

While I was regaining my composure, the worker who had been holding the ladder opened it and climbed up and through a ceiling panel. The car dropped suddenly and I was slung against the back wall, hard. The car stopped just as suddenly and I was slammed to the floor, hard. He closed the panel, climbed down the ladder and folded it back. Neither one said a word to me; they snickered among themselves. When I stood up, I noticed the heel on left pump was broke.

When the car finally got to the main lobby I limped, due to the broken heel on my shoe, directly to the building manager's office and told him about what I considered to be an assault. He called the service men to his office and, you know, they had the gall to tell him they didn't notice when I got on the elevator.

Supposedly they were so involved in their testing, they didn't see me get on. The manager believed them. He said it wasn't the first time a preoccupied person drifted into an elevator that was out of service. The service men both gave me a phony apology and left.

For compensation the manager wrote me a check large enough to buy two pairs of pumps. I snatched it and limped out of his office. I was riding the elevator back up, mad, hurt, embarrassed, crying and holding a broken shoe. The elevator stopped on twelve and two professionally dressed gentleman got on.

The tears were running down my face and both men look right through me. They continued their conversation as if I weren't even on the elevator. No concern whatsoever as to my obviously upset state. At that moment, I must admit, I wished I had the power to jerk the elevator to a stop and slam both their suit wearing behinds to the floor.

I went to the bathroom on my floor and tried to regain my composure. When I got back to my office, there were a dozen pink roses from the building's florist on my desk. The card read, "We are really sorry" and it was signed, 'Unnoticed'. I started crying again. I still haven't made up my mind if I'm going to call a lawyer or not, but one thing you can believe, I will be speaking to whoever is on the elevator from now on. Thanks for listening. I'll speak with you later. Bye for now.

7

A Day in the Park

What he is demanding of me will destroy my soul. I will become like him—a dead man walking. It was only to be a simple robbery. My thought was that this one bad deed would correct my horrible mistake. I now see that that thought was wrong; possibly murderously incorrect.

There was supposed to be money here, a lot of money, but we have found none. We did find drugs, and the wrong drug as far as I am concerned. Heroin is what the walking dead needs; so, he is satisfied and now he is anxious to leave. I need money to correct my blunder. Lord, I wish it wasn't so hot in this tin box.

The daughter swears cash is coming. The walking-dead wants me to shoot her in the head and leave. He believes there is enough heroin to make us both rich. He's a heroin addict. A monkey can't sell bananas as far as I am concerned, and my knowledge of drug distribution wouldn't fill a roach sack. His plan is foolish, but he does have a point about the daughter. If we leave her alive, she will without a doubt tell her father we robbed his trailer. The daughter is on her knees pleading for her life. My borrowed pistol is at the back of her head.

Her stringy blond is hair clumped with perspiration. It is the same color as my wife's and both of them are need of a thorough shampoo. Last month I started shampooing heads at Florene's, five dollars a head plus tips. It isn't bad money, but rock cocaine takes it right away, before we could do anything with it. My wife and I are both strung out on rock cocaine.

No one was to be in this trailer. Everybody in the park knows whose trailer it is and what he uses for. Nobody has ever been stupid enough to tip her father's raft; at least not after he set that poor brother and his wife afire. It was only by the grace of God that their little boy child got out of the blazing trailer alive. If I leave the daughter alive, I am killing myself and my wife. But I am not a murderer; pulling this stiff trigger is not in my nature.

While wiping the sweat from my eyes with my forearm, the pistol accidentally nudges her head. She whimpers and pleads again, "A lot of money's coming: that's the God's honest truth. That's why I was hiding in the bathroom. I was waiting for Daddy to make the drop and I was going get the money. I have figured out the combination; it's the same as the numbers in his computer log in 25-14-12."

Her plan is for the three of us to leave and come back after her father makes the drop. According to her, it will be over one hundred thousand dollars. This is about the amount of money the walking-dead and I were expecting to be here. He got the heroin because the daughter was too scared to lie about the safe combination. She's begging for her life, so I doubt that she is lying about the money either.

The problem with her plan is where to go once we walk out of this trailer. My trailer is five lots down and the walking dead lives on the other side of the park; if anyone sees the three of us together it's bound to raise suspicion. We three together will draw attention; the park owner's bratty daughter with the walking-dead and me—the only Black woman in the county with a white wife.

"It's her life or ours; shoot the little twit!" comes from the mouth of the walking dead. With the briefcase of heroin under his arm his addict's mind is on getting out of here fast. He is standing at the trailer's front door peeping out the half window into the bright light of the afternoon. It is scorching outside. It's been blazing for two months, no rain, just dry hot heat waves and a mighty ornery sun. "If you can't do it toss me the pistol and I'll shoot her!"

He turns from the half window to face us. If I did toss him the gun, he couldn't catch it with the briefcase under his arm and the butane torch tank in his other hand. I should throw it to him and watch him fumble and try to juggle all three items.

The walking-dead, Milton, is dressed in a pair of blue jean cut offs that he has had on for at least two weeks. The shorts expose his frog leg thighs with broken blue varicose veins, his knobby knees and cruddy caved-in ankles. His callused feet are in clear plastic flip flops and a dirty, red and yellow stained long sleeve gray thermal tee shirt covers his upper torso.

People who don't mind their hygiene irritate me. Milton infuriates me with his annual bathing schedule; at least that's how he smells as if he only baths once a year. If it wasn't for my recent addiction and current need, I would never be in his filthy company. The pistol is getting heavy and the daughter's continuous crying and whining is trying me.

If I don't kill her, I'm dead. If I do, my soul is dead. My mama use to tell me the only thing a person really has of value is their soul. And life is a test of how clean you can keep it. Sins, bad deeds, stain the soul. God, how did I end up here? I don't need a deity for the answer. I'm here because of cocaine and that fool at the door.

"It's enough money for each of us." the daughter pleads "All I want is enough to leave town and start over. I have a new beginning waiting for me in Seattle. Neither Daddy, nor this life will find me up there. Please . . . we can all get what we want. You don't have to kill me. I deserve a real life too, but I will never have that here. In this town, in this state, I will always be Jerry Mac's daughter, nothing more. And the only life I will have is the one he thinks his daughter should live. Leaving is the only way for me to have my own life and that money is my ticket out."

She has turned her head and scooted around on her knees to face me. Looking into her face, I lower the pistol. She has nerve. I couldn't have moved with a pistol to my head.

"Please, it's enough to share."

For all her crying and whining one would think her eyes would be red and puffy, they're not. If not for hearing her sob myself, I wouldn't believe the child had cried a tear. The whites of her blue eyes don't show a trace of the distress her sobs owned.

"Where can we go?" I ask her. "People can't see us together. I'm not moving to Seattle after this is done. I still have to live here."

Milton abruptly moves from the front door and walks toward us. He draws the briefcase filled with heroin over his shoulder. He swings it down and strikes the daughter across her face. The corner of the case hit her like a fist and she is sprawled out on the grimy ivory tile. She's not out cold, but he dazed her good. Her head is about a foot away from the only thing in the trailer that's not attached to the wall—the safe.

She whimpers and he stomps her in the stomach. I move to him and put the pistol to his forehead. The hammer of the borrowed black revolver pulls back a lot easier than I imagined the trigger would.

"Get off of her" my teeth are clenched so tight I feel the blood rushing through my temples. She didn't deserve to be struck like a dog, especially, by the likes of him. The pistol with cocked hammer has bucked his jaundice eyes.

God please help me because none of the hesitation that was present when I had this pistol to the daughter's head is here now. I want to pull the trigger and blow a hole clear through the leather of his forehead and out the back of his greasy head. It's his fault that I am here. It was him who brought up the idea of stealing the money in the first place. He said it was a "walk in the park". He convinced me to get the pistol and buy the torch to cut open the safe.

My wife told him about my need. Once he had that information; he wouldn't let up. He was constantly running the plan into my head. If I was sitting on the trailer steps, he was whispering it my ear. When me or my wife sent him to get rocks, as soon as he came back; he wouldn't let us smoke the rocks without hearing his continuous conversation about robbing the trailer. He didn't plant an acorn; he planted the whole oak in my mind. This situation is his fault.

"Don't shoot him," comes from the floor. "The noise will draw attention."

His yellow orbs are rolled up and focused on the barrel of the pistol that I am boring into his head. "She is in our way, Aggie. We don't need the money she's talking about. We can get all we need with this smack."

Yuk! The air around him is fetid with puss and feces. I want out of his putrid company. The idea hits me as hard as his odor.

"Take the freaking case and leave. The heroin is yours; we will stay for the money."

"What?" His eye lids are flittering. He looks from the barrel to me to back to the barrel then to me again, "Are you saying I can leave?"

Everybody in this trailer is dripping sweat, but his is offensive.

"You heard me, leave!" I didn't mean to yell, but the outburst got him to move away from us and out the front door. It's not until the screen door of the trailer slams that I lower the pistol.

Leaning on the kitchen counter, I'm helping the daughter off the floor. "You wanted to shoot him, didn't you? That wasn't smart letting him leave with the drugs. Daddy won't leave the money when he sees the heroin is gone. You weren't thinking, Aggie."

At this point all I want to do is go home and kiss my wife and think up an alternative plan for coming up with the money. Ten years ago I graduated number three from my high-school and I almost finished at the University of Nevada. I stopped my studies when my mother became ill. I was one semester away from a Bachelor's in Psychology. I should be able to come up with a solution to this money problem. Smoking those rocks and being in Milton's company has me thinking like a felon. My plan won't involve a gun or any criminal activity.

"You're right. It wasn't smart but it ended and nobody got killed."

"But I'm still stuck here with no way out and staying here is a death sentence for me, a slow death, but still death. I won't stay here. Whatever it takes; I'm getting out."

The mark above her eye will turn purple and become a knot. She's unsteady, but standing. I brought my wife the same pink sundress the daughter is wearing. However my wife would not be caught dead wearing hers without four inch heels. The daughter has on matching pink slide in sandals. Leaning on me for balance, she says, "We should leave too. Daddy will be here soon. He's always at the office by one for the lunch my mother brings."

I have no destination in mind, but we are making it for the door until we see the walking-dead backing back through the door with both hands up. Milton has neither the case nor the torch. Once he enters, he continues to back up and we stop. The case and torch are flung into the trailer and land at Milton's elephant skin feet. A white shoe and a white pants leg are seen at the break of the door. I know who it is, and so does the daughter. Her breaths become rapid.

"It's Daddy."

When her father enters, a breeze accompanies him, not a cool breeze but a warm burst. It moves through the whole trailer with his glance. When his eyes get to me and his daughter, he releases an audible grimace.

"Uh, what are you doing in here Jeanette, and what happened to your face?"

Dressed in the white linen pants and a white linen short sleeve shirt, one would think a cool breeze would have blown in with him. He is the only one in the trailer not sweating. His arms are hanging loosely at his side in his right hand is a silver gun. It doesn't have a cylinder in the middle like the one I have and his is a lot longer.

"I asked what are you doing here and what happened to your face." He snarls.

The daughter stops leaning on me; matter of fact she stands up straight and walks effortless over to her father. He is only a couple of inches taller than her about five eight, my height. The walking-dead is the tallest person in the trailer. He has to be over six two, but presently his back is humped and his arms remain in the air.

"I was walking past the trailer Daddy, and saw the two of them in here. I came in to see what was going on and that guy hit me with the torch. He was trying to break into your safe, but couldn't. He threatened to kill me because he didn't want me to tell you. I opened the safe for him to save my life. He was still going to shoot me, but Aggie fought with him and took his gun. She saved my life Daddy."

Before either myself or Milton can say a word in dispute, the loosely hanging arm with pistol raises and three zip, zip, zip sounds are heard. The first two zips caused Milton to take two steps back; the last zip rocked his head back and toppled him over.

I want to raise my gun purely as a defensive move, but no part of my body feels capable of motion. He shot Milton down. My pouring sweat and free flowing urine appears to be all the motion I am capable of. The desire to swallow is strong and my pistol should be raised. I should say something in protest before he shoots me down as well.

Without ceremony or concern he takes steps to where Milton's carcass lays, he steps over it to pick up the case and walks over to the safe. He rolls the numbers, opens it and places the case and a large manila envelope from under his shirt within the safe. He closes the small black steal door.

Without turning from the safe he says, "Thank you for saving my daughter's life. That is the only reason I am not going to shoot you in your lesbian brain. Because there is no possible reason in the world for you to be in my trailer unless you too came to rob me . . . and drop that pistol before I change my and put a hole in your head."

I immediately drop the gun. "Sir, I didn't . . ."

"Don't say another single solitary word. I need to think, leaving you alive can cause me problems . . ." He turns from the safe to me "Uh. You have pissed your pants . . . not so tough after all, huh?"

Tough, what gave him that impression? I know why. It's because I take care of myself and my wife and I don't ask him or any man for help. That makes all men think I'm trying to be tough. I'm not tough or hard. I merely take care of me and mine.

"You took a second mortgage on your mother's trailer didn't you?"

To my shame I did, but how does he know that?

"Sir?"

"Look you he-she or she-he don't make me repeat myself."

The daughter stomps her foot hard on the trailer floor and gets in her father's face "Daddy, why are you talking to Aggie like that she helped me?"

He pushes her aside and squeezes off three more zips that land between my feet. I involuntarily drop to my knees. My right knee lands on the borrowed gun. To the daughter he says, "Never go against my actions. If I so desire, I will take this freak's life." And he sounds like he will.

The daughter didn't flinch. She asks calmly, "Please don't hurt her. She is my friend."

Her father steps away from her and closer to me, "Since when do you have a lesbian friend, especially one that steals from her own mother?"

He's talking to her but looking hard at me. I put a second mortgage on my mother's trailer. The crack rocks had me take the loan three months ago without her knowledge. After her stroke I was given the Power of Attorney over her estate. The first payment came due last week. Over the three months me and my wife smoked up the twenty five thousand and couldn't make the first payment. The trailer my wife and I live in is a rental in my wife's name. My mother owned her trailer free and clear. It is all she has from thirty years of being a waitress and I mortgaged it.

The father moves his clear day blue eyes all over me as if he's summing me up and coming up with zero. His attention goes to his daughter, but only for a moment. He looks at Milton and pulls a cell phone from his pocket and dials a number, "Teddy I got garbage at the safe house, it needs immediate disposal."

He clicks the phone off and turns back to me, "I am assuming you being in my trailer with that scum," he points to Milton's body, "has to do with your inability to pay back the second mortgage."

He is silent, giving me an opportunity to comment, I can't.

"Yeah. I thought as much. This is what I am going to do. You come by the office tomorrow at ten a.m. . . . . and for saving my daughter's life and your silence concerning this situation, I will settle the mortgage for you."

I want to kiss his feet.

"Oh, and wear a dress to my office."

To get a fix for my horrible mistake, yes, I will take off my khakis and white t-shirt and put on a dress. I want to ask him is he sure, but what I know of him tells me not to; he is a man that does what he says. I watch him walk to his daughter, "Lets go, Jeanette."

"No, I'm going to stay here a minute with Aggie. I'll meet you at the office."

"What is it with you and her?" When he says 'her', he points the long pistol at me. "Has she done something to you?"

He looks at me as if he just caught me French kissing her. "If you have touched my daughter . . ." spittle spews from his mouth.

"Nothing happened between us Daddy that I didn't want to happen."

Oh Lord, what is she saying?

The zips are heard and pieces of the tile are flying up all around me. I pull the borrowed gun from under my knee and squeeze as hard as I can repeatedly. Spots on my body, mostly in my chest, are on fire. I see red scatter across the father's face and he topples back like Milton. He's motionless on the floor. I have to lie down. I go from my knees to my stomach. The spit that comes out of my mouth is mostly red. I want to go home and be with my wife.

Rolling over I see the daughter at the safe. She retrieves the envelope and the case. She bends down to get the butane torch. I aim my gun at her and pull the trigger—no more bullets. She turns the torch on and sets the kitchen cabinets on fire, then she blows the pilot light out on the stove and turns the gas on full blast. She leaves the torch on and sits it in the corner by the cabinets. The daughter hurriedly goes to her father and picks up the long gun. She comes and stands over me. Dear Lord, who will take care of my wife and mother, "Don't, please."

It is not words she answers with, I hear only zips.

8

Home Grown

It was three o'clock in the afternoon. The narrow vinyl white blinds that hung in front of the room's only window were open. The afternoon sun was flooding into the one room studio apartment.

It is a bright room without the sun; with the sunshine it beams. The cherry wood bureau, table and chair gleams in the suns light. The walls and kitchen appliances were eggshell white. The chrome sink claimed as much sun as the cherry wood and bright walls. The room held the sun.

In the center of the room was a queen-sized bed. The frame of the bed was anchored to a cherry wood headboard. The frame held a box spring, a coil mattress and Lance Armstrong.

Lance laid atop the bed, which was prepared in military fashion with a fitted sheet, a cover sheet and a thin brown cotton spread covering the mattress. Lance Armstrong was laid across the bed grinning at the ceiling.

His two hundred seventy pound, five foot ten inch frame covered a large portion of the bed. His muscular upper torso was covered by a white under shirt. His athletic thick bottom half was covered by a pair of white sweat pants. His feet were in a pair of black high top leather gym shoes. He wore no underwear or socks.

The grin across his face was due to a dilemma he had solved. The problem was his hair. He wanted it to make a statement. He wanted it to scream, "Fuck You!" He tried braids in cornrows and a slicked back permanent; but neither style said it quite loud enough. When he woke this morning, the answer was clear; he had to cut it all off. He was so pleased with the image in the mirror that all he could do was grin. The baldhead was what he needed to complete his plan.

The plan began in his mind five weeks ago, but today, September 22nd, he was able to put it all together. It started out as a thought, but with his brain as damaged as it is, his thoughts barely make it out of his mind into actions. This thought did, it stayed constant in his mind and it reached back into his past. The thought helped him see that everything in his life was connected.

He is now aware that reform school, prison and the state mental hospital were all situations he had to go through to get to today. Even the bullet that's lodged in his brain was needed for him to become who he is.

If he hadn't been in those places, and if he hadn't shot himself in the head, he wouldn't be the man he is and he wouldn't know the things he knows now. He wouldn't have been able to figure it all out, to understand what he is lacking and what is needed. If all the situations he had gone through, he would not be the man he is now.

In reform school he learned how to say yes when he wanted to say no. He learned how to go along to get along. He never liked being part of a gang of boys jumping on one. It never seemed fair to him, a boy should have a chance in a fight. When there is eight against one, the one has no chance. When he was eleven years old, he refused to be part of a group that jumped on one boy. After his refusal, his gang no longer protected him, and he received the worse beating of his life from another gang of boys. The next boy his gang beat down, he led the attack. He learned to go along to get along. To say, yes when he wanted to say, no.

In prison the lesson was similar. He learned how to think no when his heart wanted him to help others, the weaker ones. After helping once, he learned how not to get involved. He couldn't afford to be mistaken for weak because the scent of prey would surround him as it did the one time helped. All he did was say, "Hey, he's just a kid give him a break." The rapist turned on him. He had to kill the man and he spent one month in the infirmary and six in solitary. The weaker one he helped was killed the next day. In prison helping a weaker one was a sign of weakness. Only the strong survived, and minding ones on business was a sign of strength. He learned to think, no, when his was heart screaming, yes.

In the state mental hospital he learned how to grin when he cried. He learned how to tell doctors he was no longer sad and no longer heard the miserable voices that told him would never amount to anything and that he was better off dead than alive. Then he got voices that told him to put a pistol in his mouth and end it all. The bullet didn't kill him, but it slowed him down, his walking and his thinking got slower with the bullet in his brain. Yes, he was mostly sad and he heard voices, but he learned to grin when he cried and smile when he lied.

Today, he wouldn't say yes when he wanted to say no, or, no, when he wanted to say yes. Today he grinned because he wanted to, no hiding sadness today. Today he would say, "Fuck You!" and mean it. Today things would be right.

Today for the first time in a long time he would follow his plan. Not the teacher's, not the social worker's, not the voices, not the gang's, his. His plan began as a thought five weeks ago, a clear simple thought. It was during his first meeting with his parole officer.

For the first time in his life he realized his life, it wasn't his fault. Until that meeting he always thought his pitiful life was due to making wrong choices. He blamed himself for his poor reading skills. He blamed himself for joining a gang. He blamed himself for stealing. He blamed himself for being crazy. Others blamed him, why shouldn't he?

He accepted the consequences of his actions with no complaints. He stole, he got caught and went to jail. He talked back to voices in his head and the school counselor sent him to a shrink who put him on medication. He fought while in the reform school and got sent to juvenile lock up. He understood the part he played in the events of his life.

He accepted the labels people applied to him–dumb, thief, drug addict, habitual criminal and crazy. His actions, the things he did, caused people to call him such things. Lance Armstrong was what people told him he was. He was sitting across the desk from his parole officer when a new label was applied. "Institutionalized, that's what you've become Mr. Armstrong."

He didn't know what the word meant, but he knew it was bad. It had to be because she used it referring to him and everything people called was negative.

He asked the young Black female parole officer who institutionalized him? She told him the system. He asked whose system?

"Society's."

"What society?"

"This one, the one we live in."

"The one we live in?"

"Yes."

"Is everybody institutionalized?"

"No, only those who have lived in institutions as long as you."

"So since I lived in institutions so long, am I supposed to be institutionalized?"

"No. Institutionalization is a by product of the penal system, it shouldn't happen."

"What does it mean, institutionalized?"

"In short, it means that more than likely you will return to prison because you see prison as your home."

Lance sits prone in the chair. Very seldom are points clear in his mind. The bullet keeps a constant fog in his head, but the truth of her simple statement gets through to him. It's true, when he thinks of a home, he does think of the reform school, none of the foster care homes he lived in enter his mind. He lived most of his childhood at the reform school.

"But, I don't understand, it's not my fault that I think of the reform school as home, that's where I grew up, that's where I was sent."

"No one is blaming you for the condition, Mr. Armstrong. Society is largely to blame."

"What you telling me is that I keep going back to jail and prison because I see a lock up as home?"

"What I am saying Mr. Armstrong is that you don't fear incarceration as most members of society do and that could be a reason for so many repeat offenses."

"I commit crimes because that's all I know how to do. That's how I get my money, crime is all the white man has left me."

"It's not a black or white thing Mr. Armstrong, it's a societal ill."

"Yeah, but white people run society. I know that much."

A light went on in his mind that day and stayed on. The white man, the white man's society, the white man's rules; he was a Black man. It wasn't his fault. He was in the wrong society. He was the wrong color for this society. It wasn't his fault. How was he supposed to play by their rules? They were white rules. He was Black. No one explained the rules until he broke them. It wasn't fair. They cheated him and they owed him.

They owed him for all the good things they kept away from him, a good education, a good job, a good life. They owed him for the life he didn't have. He was Black in a white society, it wasn't his fault; but today, he would make it right.

Lance Armstrong rose from the neatly made bed still grinning. He walked over to the cherry wood bureau and opened the top drawer. The drawer held one butcher's knife, a steak knife and a roll of invisible tape. He pulled up his white undershirt and placed both knives behind the elastic waistband of his white sweat pants. He pulled his undershirt down concealing the knife handles. He held the tape in his hand. Still grinning he turned and left the bright apartment.

Once on the street he walked erect and deliberate. Which was a chore for him because the bullet in his brain usually caused him to shuffle along bent over. To stand erect took concentration. But today he's erect and the grin is plastered on his face.

It would be the first one. The first one that made eye contact, the first one that said something to him, the first one he heard or the first one he smelled. It would be the first one.

Mexican, close.

Arab, close.

Black, fuck.

A little blond haired, blue eyed white boy. Bingo!

The work was harder than Lance expected. The kill was easy enough, but the work; the work was much harder. Focusing on the task at hand pushed the grin from his face. It was messy delicate work. Most definitely not to be done in an alley, but an alley was all he had.

The trick was to find pieces big enough to wrap. Lance cursed himself for not bringing a pair of scissors, but how was he to know? He'd never done it before. White men knew how to do it, but they knew most things. It's their society.

The work took longer than Lance expected, but once finished the grin returned to his face. Every part of his exposed skin was right now. Everywhere he looked it was right. His arms were right, his fingers were right, his head was right, he was right.

No more misery. Everything would be right because he was right. He walked from the alley with confidence and proud. Life was going to be better now. No one would dare call him dumb or crazy. With just one look everyone would know he was right.

Now he could say "Fuck You!" without looking away. He could say, "'Fuck You!", the way white men said it. He could say, "Fuck You Nigger!" and stare a Black man straight in the eye. After all he was right now. He was part of society, no more Black man in the wrong society. He was in the right society. No more unexplained rules. He walked from that alley reborn.

He was right and white as any white man. Sure he needed tape to hold the right skin on, but he would fix that. Now, since he was white, he knew he should have used Crazy Glue instead of tape to hold the skin on.

9

Marc on Mark

That afternoon Mark Jenkins stood pumping gas into his black Fiat Spyder. The car was the last remaining item from his bachelor days. Fifteen years old, the Spyder's better days were behind it. Mark seldom drove the car, but summer was ending and he told his wife he would trade the car in the fall. His young family required a mini-van; such was life. Goodbye, Spyder. Hello, Plymouth Voyager.

He watched a couple of bees circle his feet as he pumped the gas in the hot August sun. This was the first year he taught summer classes at the university. With the second baby on the way his growing family needed the additional money. He thought about one of his father's favorite sayings, "A man got to do what a man got to do."

Actually the summer schedule wasn't bad, he finished everyday at eleven forty-five and Cynthia worked the second shift at the county hospital, they spent no money on day care for Mark Jr.

The pumped clicked off telling Mark the Fiat's tank was full. The big Buick he and his wife brought last year would have still been taking gas. He was going to miss the small cost of the Fiat's fill ups. He hung up the nozzle and went into the station to retrieve his credit card.

When Mark returned to his car, he saw a young Black man bent over peeping into his Fiat's driver's window. He didn't jump to the obvious conclusion that the brother was trying to steal from him. As a young Black man himself his own actions were often misinterpreted.

Just the day before he was uncertain of what to purchase his mother-in-law for her sixtieth birthday and found himself wandering through the department store, the security guard made his presence known twice before Mark left the store. With the recent slight of the security guard in his own mind he approached the young Black man with a smile on his face.

Marc Hopkins was released from county jail that August morning. After three weeks of being held on battery charges. His youngest son's mama agreed to drop the charges once he agreed to move out of her apartment. He accepted the arrangement because he was tired of being held in jail and he was tired of living with her because as far as he was concerned she was always in his business.

She was constantly asking him, where he was going, and when was he coming back, or did he look for a job, or when was he going back to school. She had worn him out with her demands. He was tired of her and her expectations. Marc Jr. was the only reason he stayed with her as long as he did.

Marc Jr. looked so much like him he couldn't help but love the boy. Out of his three sons, Marc Jr. was his favorite. But Marc Junior's mama was his least favorite woman. She was the kind of woman who didn't know when to stop pushing a brother.

The woman was never satisfied. She had a free apartment right next to the university she attended. The city was paying for Marc Jr. to go to day-care; her public aid money was coming in, and she was working part time at a beauty shop. What more did she want? The woman had it made as far as Marc was concerned; but she kept after him to get up and do something. She acted like what he did get up and do was nothing.

He got up and got money. Money was money. So what if his money came from selling cocaine rocks and weed? It was still money. He brought in money to the household like a man should. But that type of money wasn't good enough for her; she wanted him to get a legitimate job. The type of money he earned was good enough for his other women, so he had places to lay his head. He didn't have to put up with her or her crazy attitude.

The three weeks he spent locked up in the county jail interfered with his getting money. He was broke and didn't have buy money. He knew she wouldn't give him money to get cocaine rocks or weed to sell. When he went by her place to borrow the DVD player or stereo, the locks were changed. He wasn't going to steal the things from her, just pawn them to get the buy money for the drugs. After Marc sold the drugs, he would have gotten her stuff out of pawn; he always did.

He wanted money and he wanted it fast. The fastest way for him to get money was to take it. His pistol was hidden in his her place, so his choices were limited. He'd have to find someone he could strong-arm without a gun. He didn't usually do any dirt around her school. The school had their own police plus the city police really looked out for the brainy assholes. But he didn't have bus fare to go anywhere else and he was tired of walking.

Marc was standing in a corner of the gas station lot relieving his bladder when the black sports car pulled into the station. He grinned from ear to ear because it was a little man driving the car. A small man wouldn't offer much resistance to being strong-armed.

When the man pulled into station, he left the car running as he went in to get the pump started. Marc guessed the car's gas tank might have been close to empty, so he fought against the impulse of jumping in it and driving off. He watched the small man fill the sports car up. He was a little guy, probably one of those college boys that had been filling Debra's head with nonsense.

When the man went back in the station to pay for his gas, Marc ran to the car. The keys were gone. When he looked up, he saw the little man walking toward him smiling. Marc figured one straight shot to the chin would do it. After the man was stretched out from the punch to the chin, Marc's plan was to take his wallet and his keys. Once the man got within striking distance, Marc unleashed a vicious straight jab. The man ducked and followed up with a combination to Marc's stomach and chin.

Mark couldn't believe the young brother swung on him. He saw it in the young brother's eyes but he thought he was misreading them.

There wasn't much room between the pump and the car and that worked to Mark's advantage. The young brother fought like a boxer, he needed room to draw back. Mark executed two waist jabs to the young brother's stomach and came up elbow first to the young brother's chin. The young brother's stomach was rock hard, but Mark was certain the elbow to the chin would daze him.

The little bastard was quick. For a moment the robbery attempt slipped Marc's mind; he was back in the ring as a Golden Gloves boxer in the Park District. He took the elbow to the chin, looped his arm around the little bastard's head and pulled him into the open lot. If he wanted to fight, Marc was going to give him a fight.

When the young brother pulled him in close, Mark knew he was not a skilled fighter and decided not to leave him with any permanent damage. Mark dropped to the pavement freeing himself from the young brothers embrace; he extended his right leg and spun on his left heel sweeping the young brother from his feet. The young brother hit the ground hard, but was up quickly. That surprised Mark. With the proper training the young brother could be an excellent martial artist. The young brother threw an array of punches which Mark slipped without countering. He smiled at the young boxing brother while slipping his punches.

A crowd was forming in the gas station; attention was something Marc didn't want. It was obvious the little bastard wasn't to be strong-armed. Marc turned to run from the station when two squad cars pulled in. When the young brother turned to run, he ran directly into two officers. His momentum knocked one on his back. Mark could see it was an accident, but the officers did not. The officer standing tried to wrestle the young brother to the ground. The young brother broke the officer's hold and bombarded him with crisp combinations. The two officers in the other car got out with batons drawn.

Marc's back was against one of the squad cars. The cop on the ground was getting up. The threat was the two cops coming at him swinging their nightsticks. The smart thing to do would be to put his hands up and surrender, but he didn't want to take the ass whipping these cops had in store for him, not in broad daylight in front of all these people. He was trying to crawl over the roof of the squad car when he felt one of the nightsticks across his back.

Mark's intervention was going to be verbal until he heard the baton cracking down across the young brother's back. He'd trained the city's officers on how to use batons; they knew where to strike and where not to strike. The officer was trying to cripple the young brother. Mark advanced and yelled for them to stop. One of the baton wielding officers turned on him. Mark disarmed him of the baton without striking him.

Marc rolled across the roof of the squad car and fell to the ground on the other side out of the reach of the officers. When he stood to run, he saw the four cops surrounding the little man.

The officers ignored Mark's explanations. Mark stood in the middle of the four with the officer's baton. If one of them advanced forward, his thought was to take the offensive. The target of the attack would be the biggest officer.

Marc was out of the gas station lot running through a group of little kids when he heard Marc Jr. calling him. His son was telling him the police had his homey. Marc Jr. must have seen the fight and figured the little man was a friend of his. Marc taught his son to never turn his back on his homeys. His son expected him to help the little man. Marc saw it in his face.

Mark kept the officers at bay with head–high snapping kicks. The baton wielding officer was drawing his pistol; Mark's foot had spilt his lip and bloodied his nose. The bigger one officer, whose nose was bleeding also, stopped him. He and the other officers agreed; they wanted to whip Mark in front of the crowd. They were about to rush him, but Marc broke through their circle.

The two had the officers flat on the pavement in less than a minute. The young Marc turned to the smaller Mark and smiled. The smaller Mark extended his hand. They shook hands. The crowd applauded. They both grinned bashfully. The owner of the gas station ran up to Mark and told him he was never there as far as he was concerned.

Mark asked Marc did he need a lift. The sound of coming sirens made Marc agree. He waved good-bye to his son. Marc Jr.'s eyes were filled with pride. Away from the station an uncomfortable silence filled the Fiat. Neither spoke for three blocks.

Mark asked Marc why did he swing on him? Marc told it was nothing personal; he just needed some money. Marc told Mark to pull over that the corner ahead would be fine. Neither asked the other's name. They exchanged a smile and parted.